Refined
Cadence

Refined Cadence

By

Angela K Parker

Refined Cadence
Copyright © 2021 by Angela K. Parker
All Rights Reserved.

Without limiting the rights under copyright reserved above, no part of this publication may be reproduced, stored in or introduced into a retrieval system, or transmitted, in any form, or by any means electronic, mechanical, photocopying, recording, or otherwise, without the prior written permission of the author of this book.

This book is a work of fiction. Names, characters, businesses, places, events, and incidents are either the products of the author's imagination or used in a fictitious manner. Any resemblance to actual persons, living or dead, or actual events is purely coincidental.

Published: Angela K. Parker 2021
angelaparkerauthor@gmail.com

"Cover Design ©Angela K Parker."

To everyone with the will to outlive their mistakes.

Contents

Prologue 1

Chapter One 5

Chapter Two 17

Chapter Three 24

Chapter Four 36

Chapter Five 46

Chapter Six 54

Chapter Seven 59

tChapter Eight 68

Chapter Nine 80

Chapter Ten 88

Chapter Eleven 101

Chapter Twelve 107

Chapter Thirteen 115

Chapter Fourteen 124

Chapter Fifteen 134

Chapter Sixteen 146

Chapter Seventeen 152

Chapter Eighteen 161

Chapter Nineteen 172

Chapter Twenty	178
Chapter Twenty-One	190
Chapter Twenty-Two	198
Chapter Twenty-Three	204
Chapter Twenty-Four	212
Chapter Twenty-Five	218
Chapter Twenty-Six	223
Chapter Twenty-Seven	234
Epilogue	240
Acknowledgments	251
Author's Note	252
Until Next Time	252
About The Author	253
Other Works by The Author	254
Connect With The Author	255

Prologue

Two Years Earlier

Luke

I take my warnings with a grain of salt. Then I add in smoldering eyes and a little sweet talk. It never fails, which is why I'm not taking Dalton's advice to leave Joselyn's co-worker alone when they arrive.

Joselyn is Dalton's new girlfriend, and it's because of her that we're even doing this interview. This co-worker of hers is a grown woman, and I'm a grown man. If we're both consenting, I don't see the problem in mixing a little business with pleasure. She's assisting Joselyn with the interview, and I plan to be as compliant as I can be—giving her the information she asks for and a few other things I'm sure she'll want.

Dalton is outside, awaiting their arrival.

Owen is staring like he always does—reading me like an open book. I have no doubt that he knows what's on my twisted mind.

I stare back at him, twirling my drum stick through my fingers. Then I offer him a confirming smirk.

"One of these days, you're going to meet your match," Owen says through a small grin.

"That may be true, but I doubt that *one-day* is today," I reply condescendingly.

What are the odds that my match is here in Cane, NC, and she's being delivered to me as we speak? Furthermore, she's a journalist. I definitely can't be tied to someone like that or anyone else.

Owen opens his mouth to say something else when I suddenly drop my sticks, holding my hand over my belly.

"Hold that thought. I'll be back," I tell him as my stomach decides that now is a good time to take a turn for the worst.

I wash my hands ten minutes later and start down the hall.

"I wouldn't go in there for the next hour," I say, then realize that our company has arrived. The woman giggles as I approach, grabbing my attention, and it's the sweetest sound. I stop a few feet away from her. "You must be," I pause for a second, noticing something familiar about her. Then it dawns on me as I speak her name.

"Rose."

My brows pulled together, and I barely hear her say, *"That would be me,"* through all the chaos in my head. All I can do is stare. It never crossed my mind that my Rose and Joselyn's Rose were one and the same.

I walk over to the recliner and sit, stunned silent. As annoyed as I am, I can't stop staring with one blaring question on my mind. *What is she doing here?*

Rose clears her throat and looks away from me. Then she asks for a sample of what we're working on. It's hard when all I want to do is leave, yet I find myself pulling my eyes away from her and walking over to my drums.

I stare at anything but Rose as we play for them, but when we're done, my eyes land on her again. She's like a bad magnet—or a very good irritating magnet. I can't decide. I just know I need to get away from her. She smiles at me, taunting me from across the room, and I can't take being in her presence any longer. So, I stand, drop my sticks in the recliner, and leave the living room without a word.

I step into the bedroom and close the door behind me. I never imagined it would be her—the girl who crushed my spirit back in high school. The girl who's now a beautiful woman intent on torturing me.

I pace the floor, cursing Owen for being right. My match was delivered to me on a platter, but I want nothing to do with her. I don't care how beautiful she is or how interested she pretended to be. One letdown by her is enough to last a lifetime.

I locked myself in the room for the rest of the night, trying to push Rose out of my thoughts, but nothing helped. I can't even get out of bed for breakfast the next morning, so the guys went to Dalton's mom without me.

When they come back, I'm stretched out on the couch, still thinking of Rose. Dalton refused to let me mope, and he finally pried the cause of my attitude out of me. I told him and Owen about Rose and I vowed to myself to stay away from her at all costs if possible—a vow that will be all too easy to break if I ever get too close to her.

Chapter One

Luke

I had never given much thought to the whole marriage thing. I always saw it as two hopeless people foolishly giving away their freedom to one person for the rest of their lives. Call me crazy, but that sounds absurd. I think I'm claustrophobic, at least when it comes to being with someone in that way. My life is full of people and places, and I like it. If keeping it exactly that way means that I have to carry the brand of *single*, then so be it.

I wasn't always this way, and for a long time, I blamed the woman standing across the altar for the way I am. I accused Rose, who I've been secretly admiring from afar for a few years now. Sweet, spunky, and oh so spicy, Rose. The same girl who broke my heart is standing here with me. Well, she's not exactly with me. It's our best friend's wedding, but that's beside the point. She's here. I'm here, and for the first time since she popped back into my life, I can't run away. I have to stand across from her, smile and bear it.

Standing here, trying not to notice Rose is not working because all I can think about is her. I used to believe that she was the cause of the way I am. I guess she is, partially, but I don't fault her for it because she's also my reason. Her rejection turned me into a heartthrob, a man that even my parents could pretend to be proud of. She shifted my singular focus from being a one-woman man to someone open to possibilities. Though, when I'm around her, the possibilities are the last thing on my mind, which is why I've been avoiding her.

Lately, it hasn't been easy, though. I hadn't considered the amount of time that I would have to spend with Rose when that straw decided I would be the best man. It didn't dawn on me that I would have to practice walking down the aisle with her countless times, that we would be so close, and I would have to be cordial, all for the sake of our best friend's love.

It's just one more day, I remind myself. I'm glad this best man thing is almost over. Then, I can get back to the way things were with Rose and me before these two decided to get married.

"She's beautiful," Dalton, the husband to be, whispers in front of me.

"She is," I answer, my eyes focused on Rose. Everyone's attention, including hers, is on the bride entering from the back. This moment was my one chance to look at her without anyone noticing, and I took it.

I reluctantly look away, my eyes focusing on Joselyn as she walks down the aisle. I still don't get why they want to be stuck together, but Dalton couldn't have chosen better. She's a nice addition to our family, and it doesn't hurt that Rose is her best friend. I can see Rose from time to time. I guess it's a blessing and a curse.

I lean forward a fraction. "There's still time to back out. The car's still out front," I remind Dalton.

"Luke," he warns through his teeth, never once taking his eyes off of his bride, his smile remaining intact.

I return to my position, feeling proud. If my antics in the last few weeks didn't sway Dalton, then I know he's ready.

Despite my reluctance to follow in his footsteps, the ceremony was beautiful.

I step outside for a few minutes for some fresh air afterward, grateful for the privacy that this venue provides. Our manager, Justin, always comes through. He knows that our time away from the business is just that. Our time. Our families. Our privacy.

Only one camera was allowed inside at the request of the bride and groom. I'm no fool, though. Just because they can't get through the gates and can't see over the walls, I know they're up there in the sky. I keep my hands stuffed inside my pant pockets and never look up the entire time I'm out there. It's not that I'm camera shy, but today is special.

"We need everyone for pictures," a voice says behind me.

I know that voice, commanding and sassy. My body stiffens at the sound of it. Rose. She is the reason why I won't raise my eyes to the sky. I can't have the media seeing me like this, with a crack in my armor.

I don't turn around, but I don't ignore her either. I can't. I was told to play nice—Dalton's exact words.

"Be right there," I respond over my shoulder. I want nothing more than to face Rose, but she's a temptress with her dark wavy curls and curves to match. It's getting harder each day to be around her. She's always been my weakness.

"See you inside," she says.

I listen to her heal, clinking against the marvel when she steps inside and walks away. I relax and pull in a calming breath, preparing myself for the coming minutes of torture. Then I go inside to get it over with.

I'm used to taking pictures, always prepared. Today, I'm nervous for obvious reasons, and I don't like that feeling.

The camera lady snapped tons of pictures with all of us together before we dwindled to just four. Then I hear the words that I've been dreading all day.

"I need the best man and the maid of honor," Debbie directs, holding her camera.

Dalton and Joselyn step aside, leaving me and Rose front and center.

It's been so uncomfortable keeping my hands in my pockets today around Rose, but it's the best place for them. So, I leave them there.

Rose looks at me and smiles. I think I smile back. I'm not sure. It's hard to tell what my face is doing while focusing my attention on my body and not reacting to her.

"Can you move in closer? I'm sure neither of you bites," Debbie says.

There are a few chuckles around us, but I ignore them. I step closer to Rose, and she steps closer to me until we're standing next to each other. I take a deep breath, hoping no one notices how tense I am.

My Rose smells like lavender.

My thoughts from earlier as I walked her down the aisle flow through my mind, and I grin to distract myself from her closeness.

"How do you want me?" Rose asks with her attention on Debbie now.

My grin subsides as I look down at her, her words punching me in the chest. Rose didn't direct her question to me, but my body behaves as if she had. The answer to her question is on the tip of my tongue, among other places.

Easy boy. That's our secret. I mentally coax, calming myself.

"Just as you are, facing each other," Debbie answers.

Debbie snapped a few pictures before asking us to face the front. "Are you comfortable putting your arm around her?" She asks me.

No.

I nod yes and put my arm around Rose, my hand touching her waist, drawing her closer. Her deep intake of breath doesn't go unnoticed. Holding her like this feels unfamiliar but natural. It's like this is where I'm supposed to be, by her side. I wonder how she feels about my touch. I realize that no one asked her permission.

"Are you okay with this?" I ask Rose, surprising myself. I've never had to ask a woman if they were cool with me touching them because they're usually the aggressor. With Rose, it's different. I care what she wants, how she feels, and what she thinks.

Rose looks up at me, and in her eyes, I see that she's just as nervous about this as I am. She nods her approval and looks away. My hand tightens on her waist.

Debbie snapped a few more pictures, then asked us for one last pose. "Both of you turn to your right."

We move into position, and I've never been so grateful for the woman in front of me. If it weren't for her, I wouldn't have learned how to tamper down so quickly. Granted, it's only temporary around her, but I'd be hard as a rock on her back right now. I hope we're almost done.

I bring my hand up to Rose's waist without being told, and she looks over her shoulder at me. Debbie snaps away with her camera, and I swear the last shot was the brightest, causing Rose and me to break our gaze.

"All done. Can I get the bride and groom for the final shots?" Debbie asked.

Rose moves out of my grip, stepping away and to the side. I move too but in the opposite direction. As Debbie takes care of the bride and groom, I watch Rose across the room. My hand tingles with remembrance, itching to get back to her.

"You okay?" Owen slapped my shoulder, pulling my gaze away from Rose.

"Yeah. Perfect," I lie.

"I see the way you're looking at her. You two seemed pretty intense up there," he says."

I bump my shoulder against his. "You know me. I know how to put on a good show." *And apparently, Rose does too.*

"If you say so," Owen pauses. "They seem happy," he nods toward Dalton and Joselyn.

"Yeah. They do," I answer.

"Who knows. Maybe that'll be us one day," Owen adds.

I watch them and how they react to one another. I mentally entertain the idea, wondering if I would ever let myself get that far—if I'd ever fall so deeply for someone that I'd tie myself to them for life.

"Honestly, I don't see that happening for me, but if you're ever in the market for a best man, count me in." *Just be sure your bride is not best friends with Rose. I can't go through this again.*

Owen glances at Rose, then looks at me, watching me closely in that way he does with everyone, before letting out a chuckle. "Let's get through the reception, then maybe revisit this conversation later."

I love Owen like a brother, but at this moment, I hate him because he knows something, and he's not telling.

The reception hall is at capacity when I get there. Everyone's sitting around waiting for Dalton and Joselyn to arrive. Apparently, the bride needed to change into another dress.

I look around for Rose, but she's nowhere to be found. I lost sight of her once we finished with the photoshoot. I assume she's helping Joselyn with the change and hasn't come over yet.

I occupy my assigned seat at the table set aside for the bridal party, thankful that we don't have to make an entrance as we did at the wedding. Owen is already there, peering out over the crowd, examining everyone as usual.

"What's the big secret?" I ask, referring to the last thing Owen said to me before he disappeared. I lean back in my chair, mirroring his stare. I don't see what he gets out of people watching.

"No secret. Just an observation," Owen responds, casual as ever. "Should be interesting for sure."

"Cut the shit, Owen. What do you know?" I turn my gaze in his direction, irritated and sick of his cryptic messages. I should know better by now that he'd never give me a straight answer.

"I know a lot," he replies smartly. A smile appears on his face. "You, on the other hand, are oblivious to what's right in front of you." He nods his head forward, and I follow his eyes toward the entrance.

Rose. My Rose with another man.

I try not to react outwardly when all I want to do is remove her from his clutch. My throat is dry as a bone, and my feet burn to go to her. I almost do just that until the voice inside my head reminds me that she's not mine, that I'm not one to commit. Rose is better off without me, and I without her.

Even knowing all this, I can't escape the nagging feeling inside of me. Sure, Rose doesn't belong to me, but that guy doesn't deserve her. No one does.

Everyone knows that you don't attend weddings with a woman unless you're serious about a relationship. Is that what they have? A relationship?

I didn't want Rose for myself, but I'd never entertained the idea that she was with someone else. What's out of sight is out of mind, but this. Seeing her with that guy after being in the same vicinity as her for the past few weeks pisses me off. I know what it feels like to touch her skin, to be that guy on her arm.

"I didn't realize we were bringing dates to the wedding," I forced out.

"Neither did I, but Rose seems happy. Don't you think? Did you know she was dating someone?" Owen asks.

"No." I try to keep my tone level, but the more Owen talks about Rose, the warmer my skin gets. I can feel sweat starting to penetrate the skin on my forehead.

"You should go say hi," Owen laughs over his words, further annoying me.

My fist balls and loosens at my side. I give Owen a *fuck you* look, then return my attention to Rose. A few more hours and I can be done with her, with all of this. I shouldn't care that she's here with someone else, but I can't take my eyes off of her.

The guy escorts Rose to a table, then leans over to her ear for a few seconds. Her lips widened into a smile, the quiet tremor of her laughter hitting me across the room. Their arms untangle, and his hand lands on the center of her back. He leans over to kiss the side of her cheek then sits as Rose walks away.

My nose flares and Owen let out a chuckle next to me.

Rose commands my eyes as she walks in my direction. My lady in red. Her bare shoulders glisten as she moves. Her dress fits perfectly, accenting her curves and the sway of her hips.

Who the fuck chooses red for a wedding? It's the color of death and a sign of new beginnings, and Rose is swathed in it. She is a beacon, and she's coming straight for me.

"She's a beautiful woman," Owen says, snapping me out of my trance.

I glance at him, struggling to remain neutral.

"But I don't know," he continues. "She's a little too feisty for me."

I look away, satisfied with his conclusion. "Yeah, it's probably best if you stay away from that one."

"Doesn't matter. She's already taken," Owen says.

"Even if she wasn't, she's off-limits," I say smoothly, glancing in his direction again.

"Off-limits?"

"Yeah. You know. Guy code and all." *I need a drink.*

"Right," Owen drags out. "I almost forgot about your teenage crush."

"Hey, guys." Rose greets us on arrival, sitting two seats down from us.

I turn to look at her mouth, keeping my lips tight to keep from frowning. Her smile is still as bright as the moment dude put it there. I wonder what he told her to make her react that way.

She looks from Owen to me, and as our eyes meet, a bulge begins to form in my pants. I reposition myself to try and hide it.

Owen says hi, and I nod, not wanting to speak and risk saying her name. Her name has been running rampant through my mind for weeks. Saying it out loud and directly to her will make things between us too real. I can't be real with Rose.

"Joselyn & Dalton should be here any minute," Rose says, looking away from me and toward the entrance. "Newlyweds," she huffs. "Gotta love 'em, right?"

Gosh, she's the most beautiful sight I've ever seen.

Rose clasps her hands together on her lap, sitting straight in her chair. I'm aware of every breath that she takes, the way her chest rises and falls, and the small part between her lips. Her hair brushes the center of her back, leaving her neck open for me to see. My tongue moves across my lips, imagining them there, the taste and feel of her skin against mine.

Owen was right. Rose is a feisty one. I've seen her in action from afar, but her demeanor changes around me. She still has that edge to her, but her eyes speak to me differently.

You can't. The small voice reminds me.

But I want to. I answer back.

I want to taste her lips just one time, but I know it won't be enough.

A commotion at the entrance demands my attention, and I look away from Rose toward the disruption. The wedding planner taps her palm against a microphone, stopping only when the room grows quiet.

With every eye focused on her, she says, "I present to you, Mr. & Mrs. Dalton Evers."

Chapter Two

Rose

Luke is a sexy human being.

I've crushed on the boy as a young girl. I've followed his star status as a woman. I one hundred percent love him as a drummer.

Lucas Anders, the man outside the spotlight, is not what I had expected. He's different from what I've seen and heard about him, and I don't know how to feel about that. I'm a lot of things when he's around.

Tense.

Anxious.

Confused.

But most of all, curious.

It's no secret that I've always wanted to get to know Luke. I've had dreams of us in some very compromising positions, none of which have come true. His wall is concrete when it comes to me.

I guess I should be happy. I had every girl's dream, even if it wasn't real. For a few short weeks, I got to spend quiet time with Luke, and I do mean quiet because he barely spoke to me, only when it was necessary. Come to think of it; I don't think he's said my name once.

Luke looks at me as if he wants to devour me, but his actions are the polar opposite. I get it. Joselyn told me that I broke his heart in high school, but I was the one heartbroken. We were kids. He was older, and even then, I was starstruck. He hasn't brought it up during our time together, and neither have I.

It's clear that he doesn't feel anything significant for me, but I do have feelings for him. Walking into this room under his watchful eyes, I knew I'd feel completely naked. So, I hung onto Edward's arm on the way in. He was a good sport and made a joke about me buying him lunch at work next week. Edward's a decent guy, one that I probably would've dated if he wasn't playing for the same team as me.

Joselyn places her hand over mine at the table. "Everything okay?"

I smile. "Sure," I say. "Stop worrying about me. It's your day. Remember?"

I'm seated between her and her sister, Katie. It's been almost an hour since she and Dalton sat down, and I just realized I'd been in my own world ever since. I'm sure my food is cold by now.

"What's important today is your happiness," I continue. "What am I going to do without you for two whole weeks?" A lonely tear falls from her eye as she throws one arm around me, pulling me into her side. Her hormones have been out of whack since she got pregnant.

"You could practice making a baby," I whisper. "Having a bun in the oven already is no excuse," I wiggle my brows, and we both laugh.

"So, what's going on with you and...," she pauses, jerking her head to the left.

I glance over at Luke, knowing exactly who she means. Our eyes meet briefly before I look away.

"Oh, you know. Same old chapter. He's a brick wall, and I think it's time to let it go."

"If I remember correctly, you said that a few years back," she reminds me.

"Yeah, but I thought that this," I say, motioning around us, "would bring us somewhat closer together. But I got nothing from him. It's like he's afraid of me or something. On the bright side, he doesn't seem angry anymore."

Joselyn gives me a somber look. "Do me a favor while I'm gone?" She asks.

"What's that?"

"Have some fun. And I don't mean hanging out at the bar with Al." I nod, but she knows me well. "I'm serious, Rose."

"I'm not making any promises, but I will consider it."

"Good. Now, if you don't mind, I believe that's our queue." Dalton stands and offers Joselyn his hand. "I'm going to dance with my husband. See you out there in a bit," she says as they move past me.

I watch them as they dance their first dance as husband and wife. They look so happy, so content. Seeing them this way makes me want to cry.

When their dance is over, others start to join them on the dance floor. Owen snatches Katie up and whisks her off, and I kind of wish Luke would do the same for me, but he doesn't. Edward, being the gentleman that he is, is the one who asks me to dance first. So, I took him up on his offer, leaving Luke at the table alone.

A few upbeat songs later, the music slows, and Edward takes my hand in his, pulling me close. We talk about unimportant things while we dance, and I'm grateful for the distraction.

A throat clears behind me, breaking our conversation. Edward looks over my shoulder. His lips curve into a smile, a smile that could mean only one thing. A hot guy is standing behind me.

"Mind if I cut in?" I hear Luke say. "I've heard that it's customary for the best man to dance with the maid of honor."

I'm shocked by his intrusion. I want to ask, why now, but does it matter? He wants to dance with me, and this is probably the last time I'll have the opportunity to be close to him. Once this is over and he returns to his life, I can begin the process of forgetting about him.

Edward's eyes fall to mine, silently asking if it's okay. I nod, then he releases me and steps away.

Neither of us moves, but I can feel Luke's breath heavy on my shoulder. I expect him to make the next move since he set this in motion. I want him to touch me, to say something, but he doesn't. For a moment, I think that this is his way of paying me back for what I did to him when we were younger. Maybe I'll turn around, and he'll laugh in my face. I don't know what his game is, but I'll play.

I turn around to look at him. "Still want that dance?" I offer my hand to him.

His forehead wrinkles as he takes a step toward me. "Yes," he answers as if he's trying to convince himself.

"Are you sure?" I tilt my head, trying to figure him out. I've never met anyone so confusing in my life.

"Sure," is all he says before accepting my hand loosely in his.

I step closer to him, and we begin to sway to the music. The way he holds me feels forced. His other hand is carefully placed on my side. His movements are stiffly measured. I feel like I'm being judged with every step we take, and I start to wonder why he even bothered asking if he would be so uptight and brooding. He's determined to make it impossible for me to enjoy this time with him, but I have other plans.

I bring his other hand down, placing it on my side. Then I put my arms around his neck.

Luke stops moving, causing me to freeze right along with him, but I refuse to let go. He asked for a dance, and he's going to get it. And I'll make it one he will always remember. His eyes full of steam find mine but give nothing away. The song ends, and still, we stay there wrapped in each other's arms. Our surroundings fade, and all that remains is us. Luke seems confused about something, but he doesn't release me.

The next song begins to play, another smooth melody, and Luke's hands grip my waist, pulling me even closer. I gasp, surprised by the sudden movement. I loosen my grip, letting my palms rest at the back of his neck, his hair tickling my fingers as we begin to move again. His skin warms to my touch, and I relax onto him, letting his body guide me. I lay my head on his chest, soaking up as much of him as I can get. I breathe him in, the smell of sandalwood and ivory calming me further.

This is the best dance I've ever had, and I'm doing it with Luke. The thought that I may never get to do it again has me pressing my fingers to his skin. He returns the gesture by briefly squeezing my side. Our digits silently say what I believe we can't say out loud.

Luke's hand moves slowly up my side, to my shoulder, to the back of my head. His fingers brush through my curls, and I close my eyes. The way his chest fluctuates under my cheek, I imagine that his eyes are closed too, even if they aren't.

I want more time with Luke, but I don't think that's possible. Today is what we have.

"You," I hear Luke say into my hair, and I wonder what he means. One word. Nothing else follows.

So, I say it back to him. "You." Only I know the meaning behind my word. The way he makes me feel when

I'm around him. The way he touches me with want. The way his eyes study me with need. For the few words he's said, and for the ones that he hasn't. There's something about him, and I wish we had more time for me to figure it out.

I hear the song coming to an end, so I raise my head to look at him and rest my hands on his shoulders. Our eyes lock, and we stop moving before the song ends. His hands cup my face, his eyes dropping to my mouth. He licks his lips, and my body heats at the gesture. He is definitely not the Luke I thought I knew. Somehow, this Luke is better than I'd imagined.

Luke's face moves toward mine, and I prepare for him to kiss me. I'm so ready to feel his lips pressed against mine. He stops an inch away from my mouth, his eyes still holding mine. "Rose," he says. The desire in his voice is evident as he rubs his thumb over my bottom lip. Then he raises his head and presses a kiss to my forehead, his mouth lingering there a bit. The music stops, and he stops with it, every part of him that laid claim to me now missing. He walks away from me, and his actions leave me both hot for him and frustrated.

Chapter Three

Luke

I needed to get away from Rose. I was an inch away from tasting her lips, from changing the dynamics of us. I have to admit that our dance was unforgettable. My resistance was met with equal force, and I gave in to her. I thought a few minutes couldn't hurt. So, I allowed myself to get lost in her. She held me as if she didn't want to let go, and I held her right back. It didn't matter that we were in a crowded room or that my friends were probably dissecting my every move. I didn't care about the questions that were inevitable after this was over. I just wanted to have her in my arms, and if she was willing, I for damn sure was taking her up on the offer.

The only thing I regret now is leaving her on the dance floor. The other guy seemed all too happy to step back in to fill my space. Rose is now laughing it up with him as if we never had our moment.

I tilt my glass to my mouth, sipping the dark liquid, letting it slide down my throat. It's not as satisfying as Rose was, but it'll do. I'm all out of excuses. So, it's enough to keep me from interrupting them again and making a complete fool out of me.

I place the glass onto the table, not wanting to drink too much at once.

Owen's hand lands on my shoulder, then he removes it and sits next to me.

"I saw you out there in the mix before," comes his comment.

I stare at him, waiting for more, but he just smiles.

"Was there a question in your statement?" I asked.

"Again, just an observation," he answers, tilting his head to one side. "How *did* you get her away from him in the first place?"

I shrug. It's obvious that Owen knows I'm attracted to Rose. Who wouldn't be? She's gorgeous. "Spouted some shit about the best man and maid of honor. How it was custom for us to dance."

"And he fell for it?" Owen raises an eyebrow.

I take a sip from my glass and set it back down. "We had our dance," I say smugly.

Owen nods with approval. "Now that's what you'd call secure in your relationship. For him to lend his girl to *the* Luke Anders, even for a second?"

I try to keep calm. I hate the way Owen talks about her like she's some tool to be passed around. And she's certainly not some pawn in a game. I'm about to tell him that when he begins to speak again.

"I'm just fuckin' with you, man, but seriously," he pauses. "I see the way you look at her and the way she looks at you. My advice," he pauses again, and I nod for him to continue. "If she's a mystery to you, and you feel like she's someone worth figuring out, go after her before it's too late. We all have a past. Maybe Rose is the one person strong enough to weather yours," he says as if he can read my mind.

And just like that, my irritation with Owen fades away.

Owen has always been the most level headed in our group. He sits back and watches, so he sees what most don't. Everything he said is true. I can't deny it. I don't know if I'll take his advice, but I heard him loud and clear.

The music stops, and the wedding planner taps on the mic again to get everyone's attention. "Can I get all of the single gentlemen in the room center floor?"

Owen stands and hits me on my back as he passes, signaling for me to get up, but I stay planted.

The planner looks at me and raises her eyebrows, then singles me out in front of everyone. "Luke. The wedding party is definitely not exempt."

I want to object, but it's not my day, and I'm the best man. So, it's kind of a given that I participate in everything.

I stand and make my way to the dance floor, where everyone is jumbled together. Owen pushes me out front, and I hold myself back from punching him. The last thing I need is a garter belt in my hands. Well, not one from a real bride.

I try to push my way back into the group, but no one is budging. They're all just like me, afraid of a little superstition.

Dalton stands about ten feet in front of us with the garter in his hand. He glances over his shoulder, smiling from cheek to cheek, and I swear he makes eye contact with me. He looks away, and as his hand rises, so does my heartbeat. Somehow, I know that this won't work in my favor.

Time seems to slow as the red laced material floats through the air, and again I wonder why someone would choose red for a wedding. The color alone should warn me to stop, to look away, but my eyes can't help but follow it. As it gets closer, I try to get my feet to move, but they won't. The air around me thins as everyone else backs away. My instincts kick in, intending to block the flying object from hitting me, but my fucking hands catch it instead.

I'm not sure why, but Rose is the first thought to enter my mind after catching it, and my feet finally let go of me.

A flurry of laughter erupts from the guys, along with a series of whispers from the ladies. There aren't many here, but those that are, are all watching me like I'm the prize—except for Rose. There's a hint of sadness in her gaze.

The ladies rush to the center floor when it's their turn, eager to catch the bouquet. Rose stands the farthest away, appearing to write it off as a lost cause.

Joselyn yells, "Ready?"

I continue to watch Rose. A few seconds pass, then her eyes widen. She holds out her arms, and the bouquet falls into them. She stares at it for a few moments. Then her eyes find mine. It's hard to tell what she's thinking, whether she's terrified more for herself or me.

Marriage has always been the farthest from my mind, but in those few seconds, I wonder if it's something that she wants. Would she consider being with me without the promise of that title?

Rose is the first to break eye contact. Then someone makes another announcement.

I'd thought we were done with pictures, but recent events brought Rose and me back together for a few more. There's even one where I pretend to place the garter on her leg, pausing just below her knee. I have no use for it, so I left it there. This time, I knew better than to hold Rose as I did before, and Rose kept her distance too. If I touch her again, I know it won't be the last time. My resistance is waning fast.

One final picture is taken of me, Rose, Dalton, and Joselyn before it's time for them to leave. Joselyn pulls Rose aside—close enough for me to spy on their conversation—while Dalton and I stand a few feet away from them.

"My job is done," I tell him, throwing a light punch to his shoulder.

Dalton fakes a wounded grunt. "I'd say so," he responds, looking at Joselyn with so much love in his eyes. "Thank you for everything you did," he says, turning his attention back to me.

"Seriously?" I ask.

"Yeah. I mean, some of it was a little over the top, but it made me realize just how much I wanted out of that life."

"Look at you growin' up."

"It only takes one to make the shift happen," he says pointedly, glancing at Rose.

I'm beginning to think that everyone is plotting against me.

"By the way," he continues. "The house is free for the next two weeks if you want it."

Owen and I have been staying with Dalton while we were on pause from tour to make it easier for practice sessions. Last night was supposed to be our final night crashing at his place.

He and Joselyn are leaving for their honeymoon, but that will be their home until the new place is finished once they return. So, Owen and I are staying with our families for the duration, and I'm not looking forward to it. My family is a sore spot, one that I try to ignore whenever possible.

"Nah, I may as well rip the bandaid off. Prolonging the inevitable won't make it any easier." My reasons aside, Dalton's mom wants to surprise them by sprucing the place up a bit and adding a woman's touch to it. Not sure how he'll feel about that, but it's Mom, and I was sworn to secrecy.

I crack a smile at my thoughts.

"Well, the offer stands if you change your mind."

I spot Rose & Joselyn moving closer to us. Joselyn stops next to Dalton, and he pulls her into his side. I glance at Rose, rubbing the back of my head, feeling out of place, then drop my arm to my side. She does this thing with her eyebrow where it flicks up and down as if she's inviting me to do the same. I don't even think she noticed it, but I feel her gesture everywhere.

"Hey, Luke," Joselyn grabs my attention. "Would you mind picking Rose up from my place and dropping her at home?"

Oh, fuck, no!

The last thing I need is to spend more time around Rose.

"We drove over in my car from her place," she continues, but I only hear a fraction of her words. "Night... Tipsy... Spent..."

My thoughts are on Rose and how I'll be able to resist her.

"Luke. You don't mind, do you?" Joselyn asks again. "I would've asked Owen, but he already has other plans."

And I don't?

I had plans too. To leave this place and forget about the woman standing next to me.

I just stare at Joselyn for a moment. Then I glance at Dalton, and the bastard smirks.

"I could ask Edward to..." Rose begins.

"No." I cut her off at the mention of another guy's name. I assume she's talking about the dude she was dancing with all night. There's no way he's taking her home. Not if I can help it. I think that I can control myself around her for a little while longer.

Rose's caramel eyes snapped to mine; her brows bunched together in confusion.

"I'll take you," I say directly to Rose. "No sense in inconveniencing anyone else."

The moment I say the words, I regret them. Rose frowns, her body tense as if I'd insulted her.

"If I'm an inconvenience," she begins, her hand waving that damn garter between us, lips curving into a forced smile, "then why bother. I'm sure Edward would be more than willing."

God, this woman. Her attitude is like nothing I've encountered before. No one has ever spoken to me like that. Her fire is... attractive.

I glance at her finger with the red lace hanging from it. I'd like nothing more than to put it on her so that I can guide it down her thigh with my teeth.

"I didn't mean it that way. You're not an inconvenience. I just... I said I've got you, alright?" But it's not alright because all I want to do is hold her again, and if given a chance, I will take it. Rose has this pull on me that's so hard to resist.

Rose's eyes soften as she says, "great," and I wonder if she's aware of the plot too. "Now that I'm taken care of let's get these two where they need to be before they miss their flight."

My sweet Rose.

Rose's lavender scent envelopes me when she gets into my car. She flips her hair over her right shoulder and presses her back to the passenger seat. Her legs settle, and the slit in her red dress slides open, revealing her tanned thigh, the lace garter now wrapped snugly around it.

Fuck me!

I swallow, unable to look away.

I had spent the last fifteen minutes practicing for this moment, but no amount of preparation would ever be enough for Rose.

Rose clears her throat, and when I look at her, she smiles knowingly. She doesn't even try to cover up the distraction. Her head turns in my direction. "Like what you see?" She does that thing with her brows again, and my dick swells in my pants.

I jerk my head forward, putting the car in drive and pulling onto the highway, thankful that the cameras followed Dalton to the airport. Rose lets out a small giggle next to me, then punches her address into the car's GPS. I'm in so much trouble when it comes to her.

"Hey, lighten up. I was only teasing. It's been obvious since the day we became re-acquainted that you hate me."

Rose pauses, but I refuse to look her way. "Why *do* you hate me?"

Hate her? That's not the word that I would use to describe what I feel when I think about her or even look at her. She has no clue. I open my mouth to explain when she continues speaking.

"Wait. Don't answer that. It's probably best if I continue to draw my own conclusions. Besides, just because our friends are married, it doesn't mean we have to be anything but cordial."

There's that word again. My bet is Joselyn gave Rose the same warning before the wedding.

I see Rose's head turn forward out of the corner of my eye.

"Yeah. This is the way things should be," she says quietly as if she's trying to convince herself.

Rose is the first woman I've been alone with who hasn't thrown herself at me. She's put me in the friend-not-friend zone, possibly not anything. The thought of us not being anything burns my chest. That same thought has me prying into her personal life.

"What's the deal with you and the guy you were dancing with?"

"Who, Edward?" Rose asks, and I nod. I can feel her eyes on the side of my face. "Edward's a coworker."

"Are you two friends?" I glance her way, then revert my eyes to the road.

Rose shrugs. "I guess you could say that." Her body turns slightly in my direction. "Why do you ask?"

"Just curious. He seems like a nice guy. Like he's really into you."

Rose lets out a laugh that has my head turning to look at her and the car swerving a little.

"Did I get it wrong?" I ask, irritation in my voice.

"Now I'm curious. Were we looking at the same guy because I'm pretty sure that Edward was more interested in you than me?" She snorts out another laugh.

My brows furrowed in confusion as I thought over her words. "Wait. Edward's…"

"Yes. He's a big fan of your group," Rose answers. "An even bigger fan of you."

Well, I didn't see that one coming. I was so focused on their actions that I failed to see the truth behind them. I saw what I wanted to see and worked myself into a frenzy over it.

"So, you're not seeing anyone?"

"Nope," Rose pauses, and I hear her say beneath her breath, "unless you count Cadence."

"Cadence?" I adjust my hands on the steering wheel for the turn.

"Oh, you heard that," she waves me off. "Cadence is no one. Forget I even mentioned it."

I pull up outside Rose's home, putting the car into park and turning it off. I want to question her further about Cadence, but I don't, as I only have a few minutes before she's gone.

"Well, Lucas, I guess this is it," Rose says.

My head turns toward her at the mention of my given name. Rose's smile, bright and warm, shine a light, pulling my smile from me.

I don't want this to be it, though. I want her more now that I know she's not tied to anyone else, apart from that Cadence person who she doesn't seem too sure about. To start something with her would be selfish of me, regardless of how much I want it. In a few months, I'll be gone again. I can't have her on my brain while I'm away.

"Guess so," I respond.

"Thanks for the ride," she says before getting out of my car and closing the door.

Chapter Four

Rose

Luke makes no move to stop me as I walk away from his car, but I can feel the heat from his eyes warming my skin. When I arrive at my front door, I stop with the key in the socket. The thought of letting him go, knowing this may be our last chance, our only chance, holds me from turning the key.

I pull the key out and turn, moving back toward Luke's car. The back of his head touches the headrest then rises again. I twirl my finger in a circle for him to put the window down, and he does. I have to know what his deal is. He's been throwing me mixed signals all day.

I lean down, smiling into the window, asking the first question that comes to mind. "Are you afraid of me?"

Luke stares at me, his expression blank, but the emotion in his eyes can't be hidden. "Why would I be afraid of you?" He asks, his voice is husky and strained.

"Well, I don't think that you hate me, so that's the only other explanation I could come up with. For the way you're acting."

Luke doesn't answer, but his eyes continue to burn a hole through me. So, I try another route.

"Would you like to come inside? We could talk and try to figure this out. Be—cordial," I add.

He still doesn't answer or move, so I stand and turn away from the car, through with whatever his issue is. I can't fix what he doesn't want to be fixed.

As I walk toward my door, I hear the window wind up, then the soft closure of a car door behind me. I open my door and step inside, turning to see Luke coming toward me. Every cell in my body hums with excitement, but I remain poised and in control.

I step aside for Luke to enter, then close the door behind us. He stops just inside the door, looking around my small rental home. It's not much, two bedrooms with an open kitchen and living room area, but it's home until I can find something better.

"Nice," Luke says, looking at everything but me.

"Thanks." I kick my heels off by the door and move past him. "Can I get you a drink?"

"No, I'm good." He stuffs his hands into his pockets.

"You can relax, you know. Have a seat. I promise you I'm harmless."

I turn to drop my clutch onto the table behind the couch, and Luke is there, behind me in an instant. He doesn't touch me, but his warm breath is coating the back of my neck.

"You shouldn't have invited me in, Rose."

Luke's warning races through my body to touch my toes. My God. He's not even touching me, and my body is already sizzling.

"Why not?" I ask.

"Because you were right." His finger trails the base of my neck, pushing aside the loose hairs. "I don't hate you."

"You don't?" I swallow, trying to regain control of my breathing while his finger brushes my skin.

His finger pauses on my shoulder, circling once. My stomach dips with the action.

"No, but there's something you should know." His nose touches my hair, and he breathes me in.

"What's that?" I barely managed the words, and my legs feel like rubber.

"I am afraid," he says, his nose still in my hair.

Luke's confession relaxes me more than I should be and scares me all at the same time. I'm not sure what to do with it, with him.

"Of me?"

"Of this feeling," he answers, his hand falling to my waist and squeezing.

My heart thumps in my chest, skin heating abnormally. I can barely breathe with him so close, so open and forthcoming. He said I was right, but I was wrong about him. I didn't think Luke could have any kind of romantic feelings for me. Feelings of lust? Yes, but not this. I could be reading everything wrong. Maybe it is a feeling of desire. If that's what this is, then I think I can lock my heart for one night with Luke. How hard can it be?

"What are you saying, Luke?"

"I'm saying that I want you, Rose. I'm saying that I haven't been able to get you off my mind. I'm saying that I love the way you're wearing this red dress," he pauses, rubbing his hand over my side, and my body tingles with need. "I want to peel it off and have my way with you."

It's even hotter than I'd imagined, Luke, coming on to me. I'm wet from his words, and he's barely touched me.

"How would you feel about that, Rose," he asks, and I get even wetter, my knees buckling under the pressure.

"I... I..." I'm speechless, and that's saying a lot. I'm never speechless. Only around Luke do I have trouble forming the right words.

Luke steps to my side, his hand sliding down my back, and I tremble under his touch. He turns me to face him, guiding my face up with his finger beneath my chin. He glances at my lips, running his thumb over the bottom, then locks eyes with me.

"If I try to kiss you, will you let me?"

It's a simple question. Yet, I can't form the words to answer. My lips scream, hell yes, but the sensible side of me pleads caution.

Luke clips my chin between his finger and thumb, and as his lips descend on mine, all rational thought fades away.

His lips are warm against mine, his kiss tantalizing, and I want so much more of him. His arm circles my back, and he pulls me to him. Our tongues don't touch. Our mouths are closed. Our lips are just together, but I feel him all over. My lips ache when he pulls away. He licks his lips, his thumb crossing over mine again.

"My sweet, Rose," is all he says.

The thought of being his churns deliciously in my stomach. The hunger is so great that it hurts but in a good way.

"That was…" My breath hitches between words that I still can't seem to find.

"Perfect," Luke finishes. He tucks my hair behind my ear; his fingers paused just below it. "So perfect that I'd hate to ruin it." He smiles, and it's the sweetest, most genuine smile he's ever given me.

I get the feeling I'm seeing a side of him that no one has ever seen before, and the thought relaxes me. A coherent thought, finally forming words. "Nothing could ruin this moment, Luke. Not even you," I tease.

"Good because I don't think I'm ready to leave." Luke's face nears mine again, the tips of our nose touching, our lips a breath away. His fingertips trace my jaw, then gently grip the back of my neck.

"Then stay," I whisper against his lips. I move closer to kiss him, but he stops me. I feel like I'm losing him, so I pull courage out of thin air and continue. "Have you ever had a rose, Luke?"

He stares quizzically at me. "No."

"Well, I'm offering you one. One that's real, strong, resilient, and steadfast. One that will never wither away and die."

"Rose, before we go any further, I need to know that you're okay with something."

I pull back a fraction to get a good look at him. "What is it?"

Luke holds me tighter as if he's afraid I'll run away with his confession. My grip on his shoulder is just as firm, fearing that this *something* might tear us apart before we even begin.

"Whatever happens after tonight. If anything becomes of us, I don't do labels. I'm not that guy."

I stare at Luke for a moment, dazed, thinking about what he said. I can't be mad at him for laying his cards on the table beforehand. At least I know what to expect. His being here with me is already more than I'd anticipated. Though, I can't help but wonder why something as minuscule as a label frightens him.

"I can live with that, but I need you to know something too."

Luke nods for me to continue, his gaze wary.

"If we become a thing, I don't like sharing. I'd want you all to myself, label or not."

Luke's brows pull together in thought as expected. Even without a title, being with one woman is still a huge commitment, especially for someone like him. He's on the road at least six months out of the year. I'm not exactly what he's accustomed to. He's used to women throwing themselves at him, probably a different one in every city. That's not something easy to walk away from.

"You don't have to decide at this moment. Let's just have tonight, then see where it takes us."

"You're a good woman, Rose. A smart, beautiful woman," Luke says before his lips descend on mine again.

This kiss is different. Our mouths are open, tongues entwined, movement slow, and it's everything I'd dreamed and more.

I'm kissing Luke, and we're in the moment together. He pulls me as close as possible, one hand gripping my side, the other massaging my neck. I can feel his shaft hardening against my belly, and heat fills my body.

I don't know what this is, what we'll become, but I want him. At this moment, that's all that matters.

Luke sucks my bottom lip into his mouth then pulls away. My lip throbs for more of him. Weak is something I've never been, but with Luke, I feel it, the loss of breath, feeling like I want something that I can't have forever. I feel helpless to his charm.

"So sweet," he says as his tongue runs over his lips.

I pull my lip into my mouth, savoring his minty remnants. My eyes close momentarily, holding on to the tingles still riding me. I lock eyes with Luke when I open them again, and he seems to see straight through me.

"Do you want me as bad as I want you?" Luke asks, running his hand over my shoulder and down my arm.

"Yes," I breathe out.

Luke backs me up to my couch with hunger filled eyes. "Have a seat for me, Rose. I want to taste you."

My knees buckle with his words, and I fall back onto the couch. Luke kneels before me, his expression unchanging, serious, and intent.

"Spread your legs for me," Luke directs, and I follow, opening wide as he slides forward.

My dress falls between my legs, fully revealing one thigh. Luke's eyes fall to the garter surrounding it, and he smirks deviously. His fingers run over it, then he dips his head and captures it with his teeth, sliding it downward turtle slow.

Watching him, watch me as he performs the act, has every nerve in my body buzzing. It's sexy as hell. My panties are soaked by now, and I should be ashamed, but I'm not because this is Luke. He's a fem-fessional, and it's obvious he knows what he's doing to me.

Luke pulls the garter over my foot and tosses it to the side. Our eyes are locked, but I can feel my dress sliding over my other thigh, rising beneath me. His chin tilts, and his eyes speak to me, telling me to lift, so I do, and he removes my panties with one swift move, dropping them to the floor.

He continues to watch me, and as his thumb finds my clit and he applies pressure, I moan, "Lucas." He slides one finger inside of me, then another, stalling, his thumb circling, drawing breath from my lungs. His tongue replaces his thumb, sucking lightly as his fingers begin to move in and out of me. My head falls against the chair, my back arching, my body wanting more. Each pull of his lips and every stroke of his fingers urge me closer to the brink. I slide my fingers into his hair, following his movement, and just when I'm about to fall over the edge, he stops.

"So fucking sweet," he says, licking his lips. His words are a tease, unbecoming of his actions.

Luke's pants come undone, his dick springing from the constraints of his boxers. He reaches into his wallet and pulls out a condom, quickly opening and rolling it down his shaft. His hands circle it, pumping up and down a few times. He grips my ass, sliding me to the edge of the couch. His eyes hold mine as he teases me with his crown before filling me completely. I suck in a breath at the capacity of him.

Luke stalls inside of me, bending to pull my tit into his mouth. His tongue teases one nipple, then the other before trailing a line up to my neck. He sucks the space below my jawline, making sure that I feel it, but careful not to leave a mark. Then his hips roll back, and he enters me again at a tantalizing speed, his hands exploring my body, his mouth on mine again.

I had expected Luke to be rough, but he's the total opposite. He takes his time with his craft, every stroke as careful and delicate as the beat of his drums. His rhythm moves through me, calming me, waking me to a feeling I've never felt before. His maneuvers hit all the right spots; some I didn't realize was useful enough to get a reaction out of me.

Minutes pass with our bodies meshed as one, with Luke pushing forward and me meeting him halfway. I near the edge once again, but this time, Luke doesn't stop. His pumps become faster, harder, more urgent. I feel him swell inside of me, and I let go right along with him.

Luke wraps his arms around me, his head buried in my neck as he lets out a fierce grunt, falling onto his heels and pulling me with him.

My arms circle his shoulders, one hand gripping his hair, and I can't help but think, *It's magical, this thing between us.* I'm not sure if one night will ever be enough.

I feel Luke's lips pressed to my collar bone, warming the skin there. He's still inside of me when he looks up and into my eyes. He kisses me once more, sweat coating the skin of his forehead.

With his hand carefully cupping my cheek, he says, "We fit together perfectly, Petals."

I understand what he said, but I have no idea what those words mean to him. I'd like to think that he means we have a shot at *something*. So, I tuck his hair behind his ear, smile, and say, "I agree, Lucas."

Chapter Five

Luke

I woke up this morning nestled into Rose's bed as if I belonged here. Her back is pressed against my chest, her breathing barely visible. I sniff lightly at the back of her head. The memory of last night hits me with brick force. Lying here with her feels foreign but right. This is the first time I've woken up in someone else's bed and didn't want to flee immediately.

I wonder if she'd mind it if I cooked breakfast?

There's only one way to find out.

I place a delicate kiss on her shoulder, then lift my arm from around her waist, careful not to wake her. I slip on my boxers and walk out of the bedroom.

I search her cozy kitchen, pulling the necessary items from the fridge, pillaging through cabinets and drawers until I find what I need.

Eggs, bacon, and toast.

Usually, Dalton's mom would cook us breakfast while we're home, but it looks like that's a thing of the past now. I'll probably be doing a lot more of this because my mom isn't the cooking type. We haven't exactly been on the best terms in the last few years, but she'd never stop me from coming home. In fact, she's been trying to get me to spend more time there, and it looks like she'll get what she wanted.

I could stay at a hotel, but I don't see the point when I have a free bed at home. Besides, I'd been saving for a while now, knowing the time would come when the group would be slowing down. I'd like to have a place of my own someday, maybe even someone to share it with down the line.

I set the table for two, then put on a pot of coffee. I'm removing the eggs from the pan when I hear Rose's footsteps.

"What are you doing?" She asks, stopping at the edge of the narrow hallway.

I turn toward her with what I hope is a sexy smile. A thigh-high pink satin robe is tied around her waist, her arms folded in front of her. My eyes roam the length of her, her thick thighs, and bare feet, toenails coated in red polish. Her nipples strained against the thin fabric, and immediately I remember how they felt between my lips.

"I made breakfast," I finally answered, moving my gaze to her eyes. "Hope you don't mind." I turn back to the eggs, grabbing the porcelain bowl, and walking over to the table to set it down.

Rose cautiously inches toward the table, her brows furrowed. When I look at her, she says, "I didn't think you'd still be here," asking a question without asking.

Neither did I.

But I can't leave her. Not yet.

The thought of being with one woman scares the shit out of me, but I'm seriously considering it for Rose. Last night was amazing, and something about spending it with her makes me want to try.

"I thought you might be hungry after last night."

Rose rubs the side of her arms as if a chill has suddenly come over her. She looks away from me, her cheeks turning a shade darker.

I'm well aware of the effect I have on women, and usually, I'm a total ass about it, but not with Rose. She deserves better, so I pretend not to notice and say, "please, join me."

It's weird that I'm offering her a seat at her table, but this is all new to me. I'm not sure if there's a proper way to act the morning after sleeping with your childhood crush.

I fix Rose a plate, and she sits, tucking her hair behind her ears, then sliding closer to the table. "So, you cook," she inquires, a hint of surprise in her voice.

I shrug, throwing her a smile. "I can whip up a few things."

"Well, this looks delish." She picks up her fork, slices through the eggs, then pokes them and puts them into her mouth.

"Being on the road so much can be hard; the concerts and parties, filling ourselves with junk. The guys and I mastered a few recipes over the years. It's one way that we stay grounded. Something to remind us of home, you know? So we don't get lost in the chaos."

Rose stares at me like I'm an enigma. I'm surprised that I told her any of that. She's so easy to talk to. She has this way of pulling information out of me without asking, which could be dangerous.

Rose clears her throat, focusing her attention back on her meal. "Have you ever thought about settling down?" She glances up at me and looks away just as quickly. She fills her mouth again, chewing slowly, waiting for an answer.

"Not really, but I've been playing with the idea a lot more recently. The guys and I have talked about splitting up our tour. Maybe do a one-month tour and a few weekly, that way, we're not gone so long all at once."

Rose's hand stalls with the toast in front of her. Her eyes flick up to mine, and I see it so clearly, the hope aimed at me.

"That sounds promising," she says, then takes a bite.

I bite my toast and stuff a half slice of bacon into my mouth with it.

I know what she wants me to say. I know what I *want* to do, but it's a tall order. If Rose and I become a thing, it will force me to deal with my baggage, and I'd be dragging her through the mud right along with me. I could try to hide it from her, but I know eventually she'd find out. It's what she's good at–digging up dirt. Though, my dirt would only be speculation. There's no paper trail other than the one my older brother held on to. It's the reason we haven't spoken in years.

I finish downing my bacon and toast, then take a sip of coffee. "It'll definitely be a change from what I'm used to."

"Well, if you need help getting acclimated..." Rose throws the offer out there like it's no big deal. She finishes off her food then wipes her mouth. Her eyes peer over her mug as she sips her drink, the act making me want to take her back to bed.

"What about you? What's your future look like?"

Rose snickers softly, her eyes lighting up. "To be the best reporter that I can be. Maybe join my girl Joselyn on the podcast one day, or who knows, maybe I'll own the joint. Or start my own company. The possibilities are endless."

I like how she's so passionate about what she does, even knowing that our careers are at odds with each other. Being with her could either be an asset, or it could mean my doom. Shying away from her because of it would make me a coward, and that's the last thing that I am.

"Has anyone ever told you how beautiful you are?" I say, changing the subject.

"Well, yes, but it sounds better coming from you," Rose replies, taking my change and raising the stakes.

"Duly noted."

Rose takes another sip of coffee then sets the mug back down with her hands cupping the sides, her finger tapping lightly. She wrinkles her nose, her expression suddenly changing.

"Look, Luke. Last night was great. Breakfast was unexpected and also great, but you're not obligated to stick around. I don't want things to be weird between us. All of this kinda feels like it's heading in that direction."

And now she's kicking me out?

I raised my eyebrow; my smirk pointed at her. I get her reasoning because the more time I spend with her, the less time I want to spend without her.

"What are you doing today?" I ask, my hand cupping my mug now. A ball of nerves buzz over my skin, but I don't show it.

A hint of a smile appears on her face. "Nothing. I mean, unless you count my date with the couch," she shrugs.

"How about we do nothing together?" I hold her unbelieving gaze, hoping she'll agree.

Her back straightens, and she clears her throat, taking on a serious stance. "It depends. Do you want to know more about me, or are you trying to get back under my sheets?"

"I'm trying to get back under your sheets," I answer, and she sucks in a breath. "But I want to know more about you first. I want to know everything about you." I wasn't entirely sure until this very moment how much. The thought of walking out that door and not coming back is terrifying.

"I'm okay with that," she says, taking another sip of her drink and replacing it. "I think we should address what happened in high school before we go any further."

Not the direction I was expecting this conversation to go in, but I nod none-the-less.

"I want you to know that I never meant to hurt your feelings, Luke. I thought you were playing a joke on me, and I kind of had a crush on you. My laugh was only a blocking mechanism. I was saving myself from getting hurt. Not malicious at all."

Rose stops and stares into my eyes, gauging my reaction. For years, I thought she didn't like me when she thought I was the bad guy. I guess I kind of was at fault. I would've never approached her if it weren't for that stupid dare.

"Since we're being honest, I should probably confess that I had a serious crush on you back then."

"On me?" She asks, unbelieving.

I nod. "Thinking back, I probably deserved the laugh in my face," I chuckle.

"How so?"

"Because I didn't have the guts to approach you on my own. The guys dared me, and I didn't want to lose. I hadn't thought past asking you out. I don't know what I would've done if you'd said yes."

I half expected her to kick me out after my confession, but she just giggles and says, "Silly teenagers."

Rose rests her palm flat on the table, her pointer tapping against it. I reach over, placing my fingers over hers, immediately feeling the connection. Her skin warms to my touch.

"I'm glad we cleared that up," I tell her.

"Me too," she replies in the sweetest voice. "Can you imagine if we'd never met again? The resentment we'd still be holding on to?"

Now that it's out, I don't want to imagine it. I only want to move forward.

I curve my hand under hers, and her fingers grab hold of mine.

Chapter Six

Rose

After breakfast, Luke grabbed his bag from his car so he could wash up. Then he joined me on my date with the couch, and we spent the entire day doing nothing together. It wasn't as awkward as I'd thought it would be, considering we started last night with a home run.

We sat side by side with me tucked into Luke's side and his arm around my neck while we did the most ordinary thing. We watched movies. I didn't picture him as the type to sit still for too long, but I guess he's full of surprises. His being here is proof of that.

I've never felt as comfortable and safe with anyone before as I do with Luke, and I barely know him. He has always been my sexy drummer, even though he wasn't mine, even when I'd only known his name. I'd always known there was more beneath his surface, but I didn't think I'd have the chance to go beyond to find out what that more is until now.

Luke's hand rubs my shoulder as the ending credits begin to roll, and I snuggle into him, not wanting this to be over. I wish he would stay another night, but I don't dare voice my opinion. I don't want to seem clingy.

He kisses the top of my head, his mouth lingering there for a few seconds, and I know what's coming next. It's the first time he's done that at a movie's ending.

"Rose." Luke's bass vibrates through my entire body, waking me from the inside.

I close my eyes for a moment and breathe him in. I push myself up and face him, stretching out my relaxed muscles. "Huh?"

"As much as I want to stay…" He pauses, his eyes piercing mine, the word, *stay,* on the tip of my tongue.

Would that make me desperate if I asked him to stay again?

"I should go," he says. "I'm already a day late."

My brows wrinkled in confusion.

A day late?

I don't question him, but I wonder if he'd planned on meeting someone else last night. I hadn't considered that he might have had a fling on standby.

Luke studies me for a moment, then cracks a smile that hits me square in my chest.

"Normally, there isn't a need to check in with my mom because we usually stay at Dalton's," he says, and I relax hearing his words. "I should probably make an appearance since I told her I'd be bunking with them this time around."

I wonder what his parents are like. Are they the smothering type? How would they feel about me dating their son? I've seen a couple of pictures of them online together, but none with them and Luke. He also has an older brother, but there's not much information on him either. The only picture of him is one with Luke when the group first started. It seems like they're very close in the photo. Luke looks a lot like his dad, and his brother is a mixture of their parents.

DOL is resolute in securing their personal privacy. I applaud them for that, regardless of how irritating it's been for me. I huff out a frustrated breath at how little I know about Luke. Most of the photos of him online are with fans, and by fans, I mean women. Lots and lots of women. That's what I have to look forward to if we continue.

"Rose?" Luke breaks through my thoughts.

"Yeah. Sure. Your mother's probably worried sick," I finally responded.

I get up, and Luke stands beside me. He touches my arm, and I sense that he wants to say more, but he doesn't. He lets go and walks around me to retrieve his bag and keys. I walk him to the door, and he turns around to face me before opening it. With his finger beneath my chin, he leans in for a lengthy kiss that leaves me reeling and my heart pounding after he pulls away.

I touch my lips, staring into his eyes, rendered speechless.

Luke's thumb passes over my cheek as his eyes skirt to my lips, then back to my eyes.

"When can I see you again?" he asks, and again I want to say *stay*.

Instead, I shrug, contemplating my next words. My jumbled brain is just beginning to return to normal after that kiss. But I definitely want to see Luke again.

"I have to work all week, so…" I shrug again, and it's so out of character for me to be without words.

Damn him.

"Can I take you out for dinner?" He asks, grabbing my hand.

"Does this mean that I'll have cameras following me everywhere?"

"If you say yes," he says, following a gut-wrenching smirk that makes it near impossible to say no to him. "But they usually keep their distance."

I give his offer some thought. I'm not shy by any means, and my life is an open book. Though, it's not plastered all over the news. Not yet.

"How about we ease into it, and you come over for dinner," I suggest. "If I recall correctly, you know how to whip up a few things. Why don't you do that here? Surprise me."

"It's a date," Luke promises, leaning in to kiss my forehead before he opens the door from behind. He turns to walk out then turns back toward me. "Almost forgot," he says. "Your number."

"Oh, yeah. That could be helpful." My words tumble out of my mouth. Then, I scurry to find a pen and paper and write my number down. I hold the pen out to him, and he stares at it with amusement until I realize my mistake. "Just seeing if you were paying attention," I smile, holding out my other hand.

Luke grunts out a laugh while taking the paper from me and tucking it into his pocket. He turns to leave again, and I run into his back when he suddenly stops. He swirls back around; his finger pointed up.

"One more thing," he says, pulling me close and capturing my lips again.

My body trembles under his touch. His knee-jerk actions are so not good for my health, which makes him all the more alluring.

Luke pulls away, and I suck my bottom lip into my mouth.

"My sweet, Rose," he says before walking out and closing the door, taking my breath and possibly my sanity with him.

Chapter Seven

Luke

The sun is long gone by the time I reach home. I get out of the car and grab my bags from the back seat. I close the door and stop next to the car, looking up to the sky. There's not one drop of rain in sight, but a subtle rumble of thunder can be heard behind the thick dark clouds.

I focus my gaze on the house in front of me, chuckling at the irony. Even the moon knows when there's a storm brewing and refuses to show its face. I don't blame it. I don't particularly want to be a part of this either.

Don't get me wrong. I'm not a bad son. I visit when I'm here, but this will be my first time staying in my old room since I started traveling. I didn't want to risk running into my brother, Jeremy. He doesn't live here anymore, but he comes around often, from what mom has told me.

Jeremy and I were close once, and even though we haven't spoken in years, I've helped him out of a jam once or twice via mom. Even though we couldn't see eye to eye years ago, he's still my big brother. I just can't bear being around him. I wish we could've gone back to being the brothers we once were. I wish I could've forgiven him, but his part in all of it was too great to pass over.

I blow out a long breath and walk toward the back door. The closer I get, the tighter my chest feels. Coming home shouldn't be this agonizing.

I put my key in the lock and turn it, opening the door slowly and praying that no one's awake. It's also why I chose this entrance. It's the furthest away from the bedrooms. I ease the door closed behind me and lock it, fisting my keys in my hands.

The house is dark and quiet, apart from the television's soft sound coming from the living room, which probably means someone is still awake. I walk further inside, peeping my head into the living room on my way to the stairs. Dad is stretched out in the recliner with the tv watching him while he sleeps.

I breathe a sigh of relief, then turn away. The stair creaks when my foot presses down on it. I stop, close my eyes, and drop my chin to my chest, praying the noise went unheard, but it's too late.

"Luke, is that you, son?" My father's voice reaches me from the living room.

My shoulders slump slightly as I turn around to go to him. I know he won't broach the topic of what happened, but I'm just not in the mood to talk about anything tonight. All I wanted to do was go to bed.

"Yeah, it's me. I was trying not to wake you," I say on approach.

"Nonsense. I wasn't asleep. Just resting my eyes," he says, pushing his calves down on the bottom of the chair to sit up straight. "Kitty was determined to wait up for you. I couldn't have her losing sleep two nights in a row. So, I told her I'd wait up instead," dad says pointedly.

I frown at dad's pet name for mom. He's always called her that, but it didn't become disturbing until I was old enough to realize that it wasn't her real name. No guy wants to think of his mom as a pussy. It's disturbing, but I've learned to pretend I don't hear it.

"Sorry about that. I was at a friend's and lost track of time."

"I'm not going to throw a curfew at you, but I have to say this," Dad pauses. "You're a grown man, Luke, and in your line of work, you should know the importance of keeping your word. If you say you're going to do something, do it. Or, at the very least, if you can't pull through, make it known. Kitty was beginning to worry. You know how she can be with that sort of thing."

I frown at the name again but nod my acknowledgment. I understand where he's coming from. I should have called or sent a text. I remember how mom would react when Jeremy and I came home late when we were younger. She would ground us, but it never lasted. We'd always weasel our way out.

"Won't happen again, dad," I reply, holding my palms up in surrender.

"Glad to hear it. How long are you staying?" Dad eyes me with genuine curiosity.

We'll be here until after the new year, but I'm not sure if I can tough it out that long. Every day that I spend in this house increases my chances of running into Jeremy.

"Can we play it by ear?" I suggest.

Dad gives me a somber look, and I sense that he knows the reason for my answer, but he doesn't pry.

"Just…" Dad pauses, pulling in a long breath and releasing it. "Give us a heads up if you're gonna leave."

"Promise."

An awkward silence fills the room.

"Well, I'm going to bed. Will you let mom know I'm here, and I'll see her in the morning?"

Dad nods, standing up from the recliner. "Think I'm going to turn in too. Long day at work tomorrow." He walks past me toward the hallway leading to their bedroom, stopping just before he's out of sight. "If you're not doing anything, maybe you could stop by for lunch. The guys would love to see you," he says, then disappears down the hall.

My dad is a foreman for Heath Construction Company. Mom would sometimes drive us to visit dad on his lunch breaks in my younger days, where we became familiar with his co-workers. I haven't seen them in years, so I'm not sure why dad would make that suggestion. Though, I wouldn't mind seeing everyone again. I'm sure the media wouldn't mind either.

The guys and I have worked hard to keep certain aspects of our lives out of the media, and I'm not sure if I'm ready to break that concentration just yet.

I shake off the thoughts and go up to bed.

I open the door and flip on the lights to find that my room is just the way I left it, clean with every tiny detail still in place. My leather jacket hugging the back of a chair tucked under a desk. A football in the far corner. A set of drumsticks lay on the dresser by the tv. A black queen bed dressed in a plush black and grey comforter set with curtains to match. My room remains every bit of the teenage boy that I was. I never bothered to change anything when I visit because I'm never here for long.

I close the door and walk over to the bed, dropping my bag beside it. This is my new normal for a little while. At least, I think so.

I pull the paper that Rose gave me from my pocket and set it down next to my phone on the nightstand. Then, I go into the bathroom. Once inside the bathroom, I strip down to my boxers, lift my arm, and sniff. Satisfied with the outcome, I wash my face, brush my teeth, leave the bathroom, and get into bed.

A wave of exhaustion hits me as soon as my head touches the pillow, but there's one thing I must do before falling asleep.

I grab my phone and save Rose's number under Petals. Then I send her a message because I can't stop thinking about her and how she makes me feel.

Me: My sweet, Rose. You've managed to do something that no one else ever has. I just hope you don't regret it.

I hit send. I don't explain, and I hope she doesn't ask.

As far as our date this week, I need a day to recoup. Rose is just that; a rose with sharp thorns and an enticing aroma that pulls at my senses no matter how hard I try to resist. I can feel the effects every time I lay eyes on her, and when I'm with her, those sharp thorns prick my skin, poisoning me with her essence.

I fired off another text and hit send.

Me: See you Tuesday night, at 6 PM.

I place the phone back on the nightstand, not expecting a message since it's so late. I expect she's probably asleep by now since she has work tomorrow.

My eyelids strain open, trying to get accustomed to the light outside. I'm not used to the sun striking me so hard in the morning. I hadn't noticed the blinds were open when I came in last night, and now I'm regretting it.

I force myself up, sitting on the side of the bed. I move my palm down my face hoping it will help wake me, but it doesn't. I grip the side of the bed, pushing myself to stand, and walk into the bathroom. Neglecting my day-old stubble, I brush my teeth and take a quick shower. Then grab my boxers, a pair of old jeans, and a t-shirt from my closet, thinking about taking dad up on his offer. I didn't have anything planned today. With Rose working and Owen settling in with his own family, my options are pretty slim.

The red notification light on my phone flashes impatiently on the nightstand. I pick it up to check my messages. There's one from Petals that reads, *"See you then,"* and another from our manager, Justin, that reads, *"I sent you a gift. You're welcome."* I stuff the phone into my pocket and leave my room.

Mom is sitting at the table sipping coffee and reading the newspaper when I get downstairs. The sight makes me laugh under my breath. She's old-fashioned that way, preferring paper to her tablet, even though it's easier and she knows how to use it.

"Morning, mom," I greet on approach, bending to kiss her cheek and hug her.

Mom sits her mug and paper down. Her arm reaches up to grab mine, and she squeezes lightly while leaning into my hug. It reminds me of old times before shit hit the fan.

"Luke," she says excitedly. "I was wondering when I'd get a face to face. Still a late riser, I see."

"It's not even eight, Mom," I chuckle.

"Tsk, tsk," she says. "It's usually just your father and me. So, I don't cook much anymore, but there's biscuits and coffee if you're hungry."

"Thanks." I pour myself a cup of coffee, grab two biscuits, and take the seat next to her.

"Have you given any thought to speaking with your brother?"

My eyes snap to mom's, and I force myself to keep calm. She is my mother, after all, and though I don't like her topic of conversation, I can't just snap at her. Instead, I take a sip from my mug and set it back down, letting the warm liquid soothe me before responding.

"No."

"Well, he's been asking about you more often than not lately. I think he wants to make amends."

Anger brews in my gut, and I struggle to tamp it down. There's only one way we'll ever have some semblance of what we used to have, and I don't think that's possible. I take another drink, then clear my throat.

"With all due respect, Mom, I'm not ready."

I can tell she wants to say more, to convince me, but she just purses her lips and nods. She's tried before to change my mind about Jeremy, which resulted in me keeping my distance. Now that I'm back, I doubt she wants to run me away again.

"Is that your ride out front?" she asks, nodding toward the front of the house and changing the subject.

I look out the window at the black Escalade with tinted windows parked out front.

"Must be Justin's gift," I tell her.

The guys and I agreed that it would be best if Frank and Dean traveled with Dalton, rather than some unknowns. Justin promised that he'd find Owen and me a suitable replacement while we're here.

"Gift?" Mom raises an eyebrow over her mug.

"Security." I shrug. "We told him we'd be fine, but he insisted."

She takes a sip of her coffee. "If Justin thinks it's necessary, it probably is," she pauses, sitting her mug down. "Invite them in."

"Invite them in?" I ask, repeating what she'd just said.

"Yes. If I'm going to have someone sitting outside my home day and night, I at least want to know their name and what they look like."

And just like that, all talk of Jeremy is forgotten. At least for now.

Mom and I finish eating breakfast, and after I introduce her to Russell, the hired security guard, I meet dad for lunch.

Chapter Eight

Luke

I arrived at Rose's house ten minutes late on purpose, not wanting to appear too eager. In turn, she made me wait outside her front door with groceries in hand for another five before she answered. She didn't even apologize when she opened the door. She just stepped to the side for me to enter with obvious frustration underlining her crafty smile.

I knew she'd be a tough one to beat since I met her. I guess this is the first of many lessons from Rose.

"My apologies," I say, stepping inside.

I'm not sorry for being late, as that was my intention, but I am sorry that my poor decision hurt her. Even though she's trying not to show it, her actions speak volumes.

"I hope you like chicken alfredo." I glance over my shoulder at Rose as I make my way to the kitchen. She follows close behind me, claiming a seat at the table with a perfect view.

"It's actually a favorite, so try not to ruin it for me," she remarks behind me.

I set the bags down on the countertop, turning to get a good look at her. Her bare feet, perfectly pedicured and still adorning that red polish from the wedding, tap underneath the table. Her hands are joined in front of her, and she's staring at me curiously as if she can't quite figure me out.

I chuckle softly. "Trust me. After this, you'll be begging me for more."

Rose's smile tightens as she swallows my words. Her finger twitches as she adjusts her position. Her tongue snakes out, slowly sliding across her lips, drawing my attention to them.

"I guess time will tell," comes her response.

I gaze into her eyes again, attempting a glimpse at her soul. Even now, as Rose tries to hide her attraction to me, I'm completely aware of her, solely into her, and desperately wanting more of what we had before. Her restraint is a quality I admire. It's puzzling to me how she can give me so much without actually giving. I'm convinced that she'll be the life and the death of me. I can feel that she's good for me, in a way that I don't yet understand, in a way that I know I don't deserve.

I don't deserve Rose, but maybe she was made for me, sent to me. Perhaps she's my redemption, the light that guides me out of the dark. The one meant to fix what's broken and heal what's bruised.

"Only time will tell," I concur.

Preparing dinner comes easy. Rose leaves me to the task while she disappeared into another room. It's the longest thirty minutes of my life, but I'm relieved that she left. Otherwise, dinner might not have turned out as good as it did if she'd been staring at me the entire time.

After I finish making dinner, I set the table and walk down the hall to find her sitting at her desk facing the side wall writing in a notebook. I stand in her bedroom door, watching her for a moment, taking in her blue jeans and fitted white shirt. I can't believe that I had sex with her then held her in my arms for an entire day. It was definitely a first for me, and I vow that it won't be the last with her.

I barely know Rose, and she's changing me. Or maybe I'm becoming who I was always meant to be. I just needed her to jumpstart my life in the right direction.

I wasn't lying when I told her I was afraid of this feeling because I am. A fear this strong could only mean one thing, that I could never let her go. And that's what scares me most of all. I don't know how to be that guy.

I rap my knuckles on the door frame to get her attention, and she jumps, throwing the pen down and quickly closing the notebook.

"Luke," she says in a startled breath.

"Dinner's ready," I say, throwing my thumb over my shoulder. "Come get it while it's hot."

I wait for her to exit the room first, then I follow close behind her. A light scent of perfume wafts between us.

Rose grabs a plate and proceeds to the pot. I step behind her, taking hold of her hips, so close that the untamed hair at the back of her head brushes my lips.

"Not tonight. Tonight, you relax and let me serve you," I say, turning her to face me.

Our eyes lock, saying so much without saying anything at all.

I take the plate from her hand, and I can tell she doesn't want to relent, but she does it anyway.

"Oh, okay," she caves. She looks down at her hand that's now empty, then back at me. "If you insist."

"It's part of the deal. Now have a seat, and prepare to be wowed." I chuckle to break the tension between us.

Rose raises a brow, then starts toward the table, a low grin traveling with her.

I turn away from her when she sits. Then I fix us both a plate of chicken alfredo with a light sprinkle of parmesan cheese and a side of garlic bread. I sit the plate on the table before her, then sit in front of my own.

I wasn't sure what Rose would prefer to drink, so I bought a bottle of white wine and a bottle of vodka. I would prefer vodka or gin to wine, but the experts suggest that wine goes better with this meal, and I wanted this to be something like perfect. Something she would enjoy.

Rose picks up her fork, positioning it over her plate.

"I'm warning you now," Rose says, looking me square in my eyes. "If this is bad, you will know the truth."

I tilt my head, smirking at her brazen comment. I would expect nothing less from Rose.

"And if it's the best thing you've ever had?" I question.

"Then you may not be able to get rid of me."

She laughs as if it's the funniest thing, but I don't find it funny at all. I don't want to be rid of her.

"I'm trying to keep you, Rose," I say seriously, and the words surprise even me. I can't seem to keep my thoughts to myself around her.

Seconds pass with her watching me watching her and imagining all of the things I'd do to keep her if she'd allow it.

I finally crack a smile, afraid that she'll see right through me if we keep staring at each other.

Rose clears her throat, looking down at her plate, her fork jabbing at the oblong noodles. She remains quiet as she brings the fork to her mouth, and it disappears inside. I hold my breath as she begins to chew.

I don't know why I care so much what she thinks about my cooking. I'm sure that's not the only reason she agreed to this date, but still, it matters. I've never cooked for a woman before. I never wanted to until Rose, and here I am. For the second time in less than a week, I find myself in her kitchen, sitting at her table, and having a meal together.

I cross my arms over my chest, my back pressed to the chair, waiting.

Rose swallows, and her eyes meet mine across the table. "This," she says, pointing the fork at the plate, "is delicious. Where did you learn to cook like this?"

I let out the breath that I'd been holding in, uncrossing my arms, and leaned forward, grabbing my fork. My smile widens, a wave of satisfaction coursing through me.

"Told you. I picked up a few things over the years. Plenty more where that came from."

We share a grinning moment, then Rose says, "You're not getting rid of me now."

As soon as the words are out of her mouth, she stills, her cheeks flushing. She clears her throat, then continues eating.

"Thought never crossed my mind," I respond, then fill my mouth with noodles.

We continue our dinner, mostly in silence. Somewhere along the way, Rose commented how well the wine complemented the meal, and I ended up drinking it with her. We drink half the bottle, and surprisingly, the experts were right. Or it could've been the fact that I was sharing it with Rose that made it so comforting.

After dinner, Rose suggested that we talk, so we retire to the living room, sitting on the welcomed third wheel. We're at opposite ends of the couch, but it feels like we're miles apart. I sit slanted in one corner, while Rose faces me in the other with one leg folded in front of her.

She gives me a devious smirk, and something about it tells me that I'm in trouble.

"Two truths and a lie, Lucas. Let's have it."

Rose has given me no reason to believe that she's not sincere about whatever it is we're doing here. The way my name leaves her mouth, so formal yet playful, has me inclined to indulge her.

I throw my arm across the back of the couch, relaxing into it. I don't know how I got talked into doing this. How did we go from a simple dinner to baring truths? I guess I could stick to the low-level stuff and ease her into the heavy stuff later on if we get that far.

Tweaking my brow before answering, I say, "Okay," I pause. "My name is Lucas Anders. I'm thirty years old. My height is five-eleven."

Rose stares at me like I've mocked her, her nose scrunched for a few seconds. "That's too easy. Everyone knows that you're not thirty."

It becomes apparent that I know next to nothing about her, but I want to learn more. Everything that I want to tell her about me, she probably already knows. So, I offer a suggestion because we could both do without the lies.

"Why don't you ask me something that you don't know, and I'll do the same for you? One truth for another. Truth for a truth."

"Anything? No holding back?" she asks.

"Anything," I concur.

Rose rubs her hands together anxiously, her eyes gleaming, her lips puckering as she says, "Ooh, interesting. I won't be too hard on you."

I nod, hoping she keeps her word.

"What's your favorite color?"

The ease of her question has me wondering if she's warming me up for the big bang.

"Grey. What's yours?"

"Green. Favorite season?" she continues, with barely a breath in between words.

"Winter. And you?"

"Makes sense," Rose says before answering. "I love spring. The weather. The flowers in bloom."

So, she's a flower girl. I'll have to remember that.

"What makes sense about winter?" I ask her.

"Well, your favorite color is grey. Grey is a winter color," she shrugs as if I should know that, but I still don't get the connection.

"I didn't realize seasons had their own set of colors."

Rose grins. "Of course, they do. At least that's the way I see it. What's your favorite holiday? I think you can tell a lot about a person by their holiday," she says, thoughtfully.

"I've never really thought about it because I rarely celebrate them now. But... if I had to choose, I'd say New Year's Day. New start. A chance to be better, do better than the year before."

Rose stares at me as if I'd made the most profound statement, and I stare right back at her. I cock my head to the side, wondering what she's thinking.

"What does that say about me?"

"Well, it says that you are open-minded. That you know how to recognize your faults, but you're not a quitter. You believe in second chances. And that somewhere under that facade of yours, there's a heart."

I can neither confirm nor deny if what she said is true, but damn if her words didn't touch every nerve in my body.

"Let me guess," I say, sizing her up. "It's your favorite too."

Rose doesn't answer. She doesn't have to. Her expression says it all. She is everything she described me as and more.

"Next question's kind of personal. One we probably should've discussed earlier," she says, her eyes holding mine. "What's your number?" She asks.

"My number?" I pretend not to know what she's referring to just to watch her reaction.

"Yeah, you know. The number of women you've slept with."

"One," I tell her.

She squints her eyes unbelievingly. "You're kidding me, right? I mean, you seem to know your way around the female body pretty well."

Rose's comment almost makes me blush. I'd never given much thought to my actions. So, for her to blurt it out like that was a boost to my ego.

"It's the truth. I've only slept with one woman, Rose, and that woman is you."

Rose opens her mouth then closes it just as quickly.

"Now, if you're asking how many women I've had sex with, I could count on one hand. Well, two hands now that I've had you."

I smirk at the blush that tints her cheeks and the increased rise and fall of her chest.

"Six? That's it?"

"My sweet, Rose. You can't believe everything you read. I'm not the male whore everyone thinks I am."

"Then why do you allow people to believe it? Why not... I don't know. Say something."

"It's good for business. I'm photographed with women, and yes, sometimes I take them back to my room. But anything rarely happens. Most of the time, I'm too tired after a show to have an encore with someone I don't know." I shrug. "I pretend to pass out on the couch, and my guest can either take the bed or leave. It's the only thing about what I do that I'm not proud of."

"I can't believe women would stoop so low as to lie about something like that." She shakes her head incredulously. "I could never."

"You don't have to," I remind her. "Those other girls are young, naive, and the credit of having been with an icon means more to some than their virtue. They'd do anything for that status, even if it is a lie."

I'm curious to know what her number is, but the thought of her with someone else repulses me. However, it would probably tear me up, even more, not knowing now that the subject was broached.

"How many men have had your pleasure," I ask her, and I realize that I do want to know. Rose is a beautiful woman. I'm sure there have been many men along the way vying for a piece of her pie. It's a selfish thought, but I hope her number doesn't outweigh mine.

"Before you, only one," she answers, closing her eyes for a moment. When she opens them again, there's a sadness about her, a weakened smile confirming my assumption.

Whoever crossed her mind hurt her, and she's trying to hide it. I want to pull her into my arms, hold her tight, and tell her that everything's going to be alright now that she's with me.

I'm just getting to know Rose, and I know there are many things about her life that I don't yet have the right to know, but I have to. I feel protective of her.

"Did you love him?"

"I thought I did," she says with a sigh. "But we weren't the right fit. We didn't want the same things. So, he left." She blows out a long breath, and I can tell that whatever happened between them took something from her.

"Come here," I tell her, tired of the distance between us. I need to feel her, for her to lay her pain on me. Rose moves from her end of the couch to mine, and I open my arms to her. She sits across my lap and wraps her arms around my neck. She lays her head on my shoulder, and we stay that way for a long while.

I've never felt closer to any other woman as I do with Rose. The thought of disappointing her as the last guy did, lurks just under the surface, trying to convince me that I can't do this. But there's an even deeper feeling that overrides the last. I want so badly to be what she needs. I feel that with everything that I am. Whatever this thing is between us; I can't just let it go.

I kiss her forehead, the warmth of it giving me a strength I didn't know I could possess.

"My sweet, Rose," I whisper against her skin. So many petals, and I plan to pluck them away one by one.

Chapter Nine

Luke

It's been two nights since I forced myself to leave Rose's home. Aside from respecting my parent's wishes, Rose deserves better than stolen kisses and one-night stands. I don't know much about relationships, but I do know that the best ones don't just happen. They're built. And if I'm honest with myself, I want to build something with Rose. So, I left her with the promise of seeing her again tonight.

"How's it been, being back home?" Owen asks.

I haven't seen Owen since the wedding, with both of us settling in with our families. So, I called him to catch up, among other reasons.

"It's been fine, and I'm trying like hell to keep it that way," I respond.

"So, no word from Jeremy?"

My secret is no secret to the guys. We shared just about everything until Dalton met Josie, and their secrets became their own. I'm not mad at the guy, though. Being with Rose has me wanting to do the same thing.

"He keeps in contact with my parents, which is why I asked to come over. Dad warned me that he was visiting today."

As soon as I found out the bad news, I made the call to Owen, and he told me to come on over. We've been camped out in his man cave above his parent's garage ever since, eating popcorn and watching basketball reruns.

I should've taken him up on his offer to stay with him, but accepting didn't feel right since I hardly know his parents. I've met them a few times, but I don't know them. They're nice people, just a different brand of family. Owen seems to be cut from a different cloth compared to his parents.

"You know you're bound to run into him sooner or later, right?"

I give Owen a side-eyed glance as if my mess is his fault.

"I know," I say with a sigh. "It's inevitable. Jeremy's been checking in on our parents while I was away, and he's not going to stop just because I showed up. I'd be a fool even to think about it."

"My offer still stands if you want to crash here," Owen says.

"Thanks, man. I appreciate it."

"I meant to ask you. How did things go with Rose? You took her home after the wedding, right?" Owen smirks and throws popcorn into his mouth.

The mention of Rose's name gives me pause. I don't want to talk about it, but trying to hold back information from Owen is like pulling your own tooth with only two fingers. It's doable, but it takes a lot more effort than just letting it fall out on its own.

"Yeah, I took her home."

"And?" Owen leans forward, his hand moving to his mouth again.

I look at him, straight-faced, trying not to let my emotions get the best of me. I press my back against the chair, pretending to focus on the tv.

"A gentleman never tells."

"You are not a gentleman, Luke." I pick up a pillow and toss it at him, and he ducks to miss it. "Besides, that's not what I'm asking."

"What are you asking?" I say, toying with him.

"Did she say anything about what happened when we were younger?"

"We talked," I say vaguely, my eyes still fixed on the screen.

"So, you fucked her?" Owen asks seriously.

I blanch at his blatant choice of words. He makes it seem as if Rose is just some random girl, but that's not who she is at all. What we did wasn't just a simple fuck. There was a connection between us that I've never had with anyone.

I turn my gaze toward him. "It wasn't like that. Rose is," I pause, trying to find the right words without giving too much away. "She's... different. Not what I expected," I explain.

"Hmm, I see," Owen drags out.

"You see what?"

"You took my advice."

"And what advice was that?"

"To recognize what was right in front of you all along," he says with a shrug.

"I hate you," I spew untrue words, laughing. Owen's not wrong, though.

"You should listen when I say profound shit like that," Owen gloats.

"I don't know about profound, but there is some truth to it," I admit.

Owen leans back, putting a finger to his temple. "I detect wedding bells and bab..."

"Don't even finish that sentence. We're not there yet," I say. *But the idea is growing on me.*

"When do you see her again?"

"A few hours from now." And I can't wait to get my hands on her again. It's only been two days, and I miss her already. The thought of being hooked on anything was repulsive until I met Rose. She's the sweetest drug.

"Can I offer you some more profound advice?" Owen asks, and we both smile before turning serious again.

"Pretty sure you're gonna say it anyway, so..." I trail off, motioning for him to continue.

"Do you remember the moment you laid eyes on her again?"

"Yeah, I was pissed," I responded with a grin. "All over a misunderstanding."

"Well, sometimes what we see as truth can blind us to what really is. I could tell that Rose felt something for you that day, given her reaction when you rudely walked out of the room. It's obvious that you're into her too, but she doesn't strike me as a crotch hopper or someone who'd put up with that type of behavior."

I let out a laugh at his choice of words. "I know. She told me."

"If you're going to pursue her, be sure you're ready to go down that road because once you do, it only makes things more complicated. Hurt is hurt, but it doesn't hit quite as hard in the beginning."

I get what Owen's saying, but. "Wait, weren't you the one who put the idea in my head in the first place?"

"True, but there's a time for everything, and you need to figure out if this is your time. She's Joselyn's best friend," he finishes.

He's right. If I screw things up with Rose, it could drive a wedge between the guys and me, and that's the last thing that I want. But I can't walk away from Rose. She's the best thing in my life.

"Understood," I tell Owen, respecting his opinion. He never speaks without reason. So, I value his words when he does. He's a good friend—a wise man.

I knock on Rose's door, and she answers a few moments later. Seeing her after my conversation with Owen only confirms what I'd been thinking all along. There's only one direction I want to take with Rose, and that's forward, whatever that means.

"Hi," she says, attempting to step aside for me to enter when I grab her wrist.

"Will you take a drive with me? I'd like to take you out."

Rose glances over my shoulder, squinting her eyes in thought. "In public?"

"Yes and no. I found a house on a private beach for the weekend. I thought it could be a sort of baby step to us being seen in public. To ease you into it." *And me too.* I think to myself.

I'm used to being photographed with women, but it'll be different with Rose. She'll be in all of the ones that matter to me.

"A house? We'll be alone all weekend?" She asks, and it's not fear in her voice that I hear, but rather uncertainty.

"It's a big house. Plenty of room for you to dodge me if you need to." I smile, trying to ease her mind a little.

Rose stares at me for a long moment, then she smiles and says, "Okay. Wanna come inside while I pack a bag?"

I follow her inside and close the door behind me. I sit down on the couch while she gathers her things. It's crazy. Her place feels more like home to me than the one where I grew up. I stare down the short hallway after Rose. I'm sure it has a lot to do with the person in it.

I lay my head back on the couch, staring up at the ceiling, letting my thoughts run wild. On one side, I'm certain that this is what I want, that with her is where I belong. On the other, I'm certain that I'll find a way to screw this up and break her heart. I doubt that I deserve her and that I'll be no better than the last guy.

I blow out a deep breath, still blinking up at the ceiling. Thinking was so much easier before Rose came and filled every vacant spot. I can't even escape her in my dreams. She's in every thought, good and bad. Everything that affects me will affect her too. The weight of it all is so worth trying with her, though.

"Ready." Rose's cheery voice causes me to jump, and I sit straight up on the couch and look at her. She pats the bag at her hip, her smile lighting the whole room.

I hide my thoughts behind a smile, hoping she can't see the torment I've been putting myself through. She's the most beautiful woman in my eyes. I can't fathom how someone could ever hurt her or let her go.

I stand and walk over to her, removing the bag from her shoulder and placing it on mine. I rub my hands down her arms while gazing into her eyes. With my heart nearly beating out of my chest, I say, "Let's go." My hand lands gently on her back as I escort her outside.

"New guy?" Rose questions, nodding toward the waiting SUV.

"Yeah. Temporarily. Justin's idea. Name's Russell," I explain.

Following my mom's lead, with Russell escorting me when I go out, I've gotten to know a little bit about him in the past few days. His mother and father died when he was young. He's twenty-nine years old. Though, you couldn't tell by looking at him with his tall frame and muscled body. He prefers to be single because of his line of work, which is a relief to me. I always disliked the idea of someone being hurt because of me. He's an all-around good guy who loves what he does. I've even thought about talking to Justin about something more permanent for the guy.

"You'll like him," I tell Rose.

She glances up at me before getting inside the car, and I catch a glimpse of the trust she's placed in my hands. I grab ahold of it, letting it absorb into my skin.

We settle in the back seat with Rose behind Russell and me at the opposite door. I'm finding it hard to turn my eyes away from her, and all I want to do is pull her closer to me. Rose clears her throat then faces front, breaking contact. Her palm is on the seat beside her, one finger tapping against it. I reach over and grab her hand, entwining our fingers. Rose sucks in a breath, her eyes closing then opening again. Then she relaxes, and the corner of her lips turn up into a small smile as her fingers tighten around mine.

I can feel it, the connection growing stronger between us. If I can't have her close on the ride over, this is the next best thing.

Chapter Ten

Rose

I feel like I'm in a dream every time I'm with Luke—one that I don't want to wake from. If the day ever comes that I'm snatched out of it, I know I'll be ruined and my heart left in shambles.

To be honest, I didn't think Luke would still want me after that first night, but he's still here granting tender kisses and holding my hand on car rides. And if he doubts what we're doing or where we're headed, he hides it well.

Please don't let this be a dream.

"So, Russell's going to take the room off of the kitchen. The other rooms and bathroom are down the hall," Luke explains after we step into the beach house.

"You've been here before?" I question.

"I took the virtual tour," he smiles, rubbing the back of his neck. "I wanted to make an impression."

I smile back at him. If he only knew what I was thinking. I don't need a fancy beach house to be impressed. Luke showing up and taking the time to get to know me was impressive enough. The fact that he wanted to do something nice for me is just icing on the cake. There's so much more than I imagined beneath my hard-bodied drummer.

"Thank you." I reach up and touch his cheek. "Now, where do we sleep?" I ask, a wink haphazardly slipping through.

"Are you sure you don't want to sleep alone? There's plenty of room."

Luke's hand moves back to his neck, and it's adorable how nervous he seems. I let out a girlish giggle, thinking about my reaction to him on the ride over. We have a certain level of forwardness and have acted out of character at one point or another. When one of us shrinks, the other shines. It's like we're passing the bravery wand back and forth between us, and maybe that's why our attraction is so strong. We know when to give and when to take.

The nearly week-long drought that I've had with Luke seems so much longer than the one before him that lasted for years. Even if the drought doesn't end tonight, I'll feel so much better with him sleeping next to me.

"I'm sure," I say, decidedly.

Once we settle into our room, Luke grabs a blanket and asks me to walk down to the beach with him. Luke holds the blanket in one arm, and we walk hand-in-hand through the sand toward the water, stopping about twenty feet away. There are two outlines further down the landing, barely visible from where we are, but Luke and I are otherwise alone.

Luke fans the blanket, letting it settle onto the ground, then we sit facing the water. I stretch my legs out in front of me, crossing them at the ankle, my body braced against my outstretched hands behind me. Luke sits close to me, one leg bent in my direction, the other bent toward the sky. The sun is just above the horizon, staring back at us. It's a beautiful sight to see.

"Beautiful," I whisper. "I've never seen a live sunset before."

"We could do it again tomorrow if you want," Luke says next to me.

I can't bring myself to look at him. My feelings are too raw, and I know if I do, I'll want to kiss him.

"No one's ever done anything like this for me before. I'm not used to this," I say, moving my hand between us. "Genuine intimacy. Having someone look at me the way you do. You're a true wonder, Lucas."

Luke leans in close to my ear and whispers, "You're my wonder, Rose. I'm just sorry it took us so long to find each other." His fingers brush across my cheek, then move my hair over my shoulder. His warm breath wafts over my skin, sending a delicious chill through me.

Lucas Anders, whispering sweet nothings in my ear. I close my eyes and soak up the moment. I'm still hesitant to look at him because I want his lips on mine now more than ever.

When I thought of us together before, it wasn't like this at all. I could fall in love with Luke effortlessly. I know it, but that's not what scares me. What scares me is the thought that he may not offer love in return. What if his feelings for me stop at infatuation?

"What are you thinking?" Luke asks, breaking me from my thoughts.

I open my eyes, finally risking a look at him. I can't possibly tell him what I was thinking. I can't tell him that he's the sweetest, most caring man I know—that he's slowly finding a place in my heart. So, I keep it simple.

"I'm thinking about how perfect the weather is. The calm of the ocean. How even a beast like the sun has a side to it that can be adored and admired." Luke is a lot like the sun, but I keep that part to myself.

The tip of Luke's nose traces the outline of my ear. "What else?"

"I'm thinking about how much I enjoy being with you."

His lips barely touch the side of my neck as his hand slips beneath the hair at my back, his thumb making tiny circles at the base of my neck. "And."

My heart races, and my skin warms from the inside out. I'm trying hard to keep inside all that I want to say, but Luke's actions fight against me. The invisible chord between us is stretched to its limits, and I feel as if I might break apart at any second.

"I'm thinking about how good your hands feel against my skin." My words are a confession that I didn't intend to spill.

His other hand comes up to rest on my cheek, and he guides my head to face him. I look down at his lips, the urge to kiss him so prominent that it hurts to hold back.

"Look into my eyes, Rose," Luke insists, and I comply.

Our eyes connect. The tips of our noses touch, and our lips are a hair away from one another.

"What do you want from me, Luke?" The question tumbles from my mouth. I'm the most vulnerable that I've ever been, and at this moment, I recognize that I'm the giver, and he is the taker. I would do just about anything he asked, but I want him to give me a sign. A sign that this is more than a fleeting season. That what we're building ends in forever.

"I want you, Rose. With all of your petals. All of your thorns. I want the sweet nectar of your center and the threat of your pollen. I want all of you," Luke says.

I suck in a breath then hastily release it, finding it hard to breathe. In the next breath, Luke kisses me, claiming what little air I have left. As he takes my breath away, I wonder how every kiss and every touch can mean everything, every time he does it.

When the need to breathe becomes too much, I place my palm on his chest and force myself away from his lips. Luke's heart is beating rapidly against my palm. His eyes smolder into mine as I struggle to catch air. Even something as simple as swallowing is hard with him staring at me the way he is.

I turn my head toward the vanishing sun, needing a distraction from what just happened, but it doesn't offer much assistance. It only reminds me of the guy sitting next to me—the softer side of Luke. I close my eyes and breathe slowly, taking in the salty air and gripping the blanket next to me. I grip it tightly, searching for solid ground again.

I open my eyes to face the last glow from the sun. Then I face Luke. This moment with him will be branded into my memory forever.

We sit in silence until the moonlight and stars replace the sun. I turn my head to the sky, wishing that we have more of these moments together. I need this to be as real as it feels. I'm treading a dangerous line between friendship and love, and I want so badly for him to walk that line with me, for us to arrive at the same end. I can't just come out and say as much, though.

Luke never said he didn't want to fall in love, only that he didn't want titles, but still. I feel like I'd be breaking some sort of code if I admit my feelings to him. I need to clear my head.

Conversation.

That would help.

Diving into other people's business usually does.

I crisscross my legs in front of me and grip my ankles with my hands.

"So… You don't talk much about your family. What are they like?"

Luke tenses at the mention of his family, his eyes taking on a brief fiery glow. I'm not sure if it's directed at me or if there's some underlying meaning to his reaction. If he were anyone else, I'd try to pry it out of him, but Luke isn't one of my sources.

"It's okay. You don't have to answer that. I shouldn't have asked." I turn away from him, a momentary chill grazing my skin. "Leave it to me to ruin a mood," I say quietly.

Luke clears his throat, placing his hand on my thigh. "It's not… You didn't do anything wrong by asking. It's just..." He's quiet for a moment, then, "My family is complicated."

I look his way again. There's a vulnerability about him, and I can see that he wants to let it out, but he's hesitant. I would be too if I were conversing with a journalist.

I place my hand over his hand on my leg. "Luke, I want you to know that being with you is not work for me. I do believe some things should be off-limits. I would never exploit you for personal gain. That's not what we are. At least I hope not. And there's no rush. Whenever you're ready, or if you're ever ready, I'm here."

Luke visibly relaxes, and I along with him. Hopefully, my words hit him the right way because I meant what I said.

"My mother is a part-time teacher," he begins. "And my father is a foreman at a construction company."

I wait for Luke to mention his brother, but he doesn't, so I inquire about his parents.

"Are you close with your parents?"

Luke's hand tightens on my leg beneath my hand. Then he pulls his hand away. He brushes my cheek with the back of his fingers. I don't even think he realizes he's done it. Almost like the gesture was a sign of trust.

"We're not as close as before or as close as I would like, but I believe we'll get there eventually."

His words are sincere. There's no anger in his tone when he speaks of them, but there is a hint of sadness.

"Growing up puts things in perspective," I say, and I don't know why those words came out of my mouth. Maybe he needed to hear them, or perhaps I did. I don't know. I'm close to my parents, but I don't see them as often as I should. We've been surviving mostly on phone calls and text messages. Luke's apparent sadness over his parents makes me appreciate mine even more.

"Yeah," Luke agrees. "But sometimes it takes some of us longer to find peace," he pauses. "I had lunch with my father a few days ago. It reminded me of old times," he smiles. "Before…" He runs his hand over my arm, then leans forward and kisses the side of my head. "We should go inside," he says abruptly.

"Okay. Sure," I agree.

Luke stands and offers me his hand to help me up. I step off the blanket and watch him while he fans the sand off it and folds it into a neat rectangle. As we walk back to the house, I wonder what happened with his family that's so unspeakable and causes him so much grief. I'm hoping, with time, he'll let me in.

"Why don't you get comfortable while I whip us up something to eat," Luke suggests once we're inside.

"Another one of your fancy dishes?" I quirk a brow.

Luke laughs, dropping the blanket into the washer. "Not tonight. I'm afraid all I brought along for the ride is bread, jelly, peanut butter, and a few slices of ham and cheese." He walks over to me, pulling me into his arms, and kisses the side of my head. "Promise I'll make it up to you tomorrow, but for now, what's your poison?" He asks me.

"Hmm, so many choices," I tease. "I hope you brought something to drink too because peanut butter and jelly is sounding pretty good right now."

"One nut-berry sandwich coming up." He gives me a peck on my lips.

His choice of words forces a chuckle out of me. "You know, you make the simplest things sound so much better, and the most common actions ten times greater."

"Glad I could be of assistance."

I leave Luke to go freshen up as he focuses on dinner.

We eat on the couch while watching tv, and wash the dishes together after we finish. Russell only emerged once during the whole ordeal to grab a ham sandwich before leaving us alone again. I almost asked Russell to join us because I sort of feel for the guy, living such a solitary life, but the selfish part of me wouldn't budge. I don't want to share this time with anyone but Luke.

"I'm going to turn in for the night. It's been a long day. Thank you for all of this," I tell Luke.

"No need to thank me. I like doing nice things for you, Rose." My heart squeezes at his confession. "Now, let's get you to bed before you break."

I smile at his comment. *The only thing that could break me is losing you.*

Luke walks me to our bedroom hand-in-hand, and my mind is crowded with thoughts. My nerves teeter between coy and brazen as I change into a black and red teddy. Luke strips down to his boxers, and I move in front of him. When I look into his eyes, brazen wins, and I tip up to meet his lips. Luke falls in line, kissing me back, but only for a few seconds before he pulls away.

"Rose, wait. I don't want to move too fast."

"You're not moving too fast."

"I don't want you to think that I want you for your body. I mean, I do want your body, but..."

"Why would I think a thing like that?"

His nose tickles the outside of my ear. "Because whenever I'm around you, all I want to do is touch you, and hold you, and kiss you. But I need you to know that I want so much more than that. I want to know the you that no one else does."

"You do realize we can do both, right? We can be," *Lovers and friends,* I paused in thought, not wanting to let a title slip through. "We can get to know each other in more ways than one, all at the same time, Luke."

"I'm trying to do the right thing here," he says. "To give you the part of me that no one knows."

"Trust me. You're doing all of the right things, Luke. And you don't have to be anyone but who you are with me."

"Truth for a truth?" Luke questions.

"Truth," I nod.

"I've never felt this way about anyone before."

"Neither have I." I loved the last guy, but this feels different, more intense, and something completely indescribable.

"You inspire me to be a better man." Luke fingers the hair behind my ear.

"I'm falling in love with you." The words fall from my lips so easily, and I don't regret them at all. It doesn't matter if he says it back to me or if they cause him to shrink away. It's my truth, and if I'm honest, I've been falling in love with Luke since our first practice walk down the aisle—maybe even before then.

Luke doesn't confess his love for me, but the way his eyes bore into mine speaks volumes. He cups my cheeks in his palms, his lips descending on mine in a passionate kiss that turns my legs to jello. He scoops me up in his arms and carries me to bed, climbing in after me.

I watch as Luke rolls the rubber down the length of him with expert speed. Then, I spread my thighs for him to slip inside of me. My breath hitches as I take in the full measure of him. He fits just as perfectly as the last time and feels even better.

Luke pauses, his eyes meeting mine. "How can I ever resist you?" He pulls back slowly, his crown still fully emerged. "You feel so...," He enters me again, a soft throb vibrates against my walls. "Fucking good." I feed his need, arching my hips to meet him, and his pace picks up as we both find our rhythm.

"Yes," I moan as my fingers slide across the sweaty skin of his back, trying to gain friction.

My moan seems to urge him to push harder, dig deeper. "Please," I cry out, not wanting him to stop. "Don't stop."

Luke pours our past few days apart into me, and I take it, letting it drive me, drive us both. My heart hammers in my chest as he continues to move, beads of sweat breaking out on my skin. I'm attuned to everything that he's offering. The way his arms tighten within my grip. His pecks pulling together and moving apart. His thumb pressed to the spot behind my knee as he grips my leg over his shoulder. The thick veins stretched against the skin of his neck. His teeth biting his lower lip. His purposeful gaze. Everything about him in this moment in time is fashioned for me.

He owns my body, and he knows it.

Luke continues, his movements slowing slightly, taking me over the edge. I ride the wave of his orgasm, my body a mess of pulsing liquid until I fall. I cry out his name, "Luke," as he grunts, driving into me and finding his release.

Afterward, my head lay on Luke's chest, listening to his erratic heartbeats while he rubs his hand up and down my arm.

I can't imagine how anything will ever top what we just shared or how anyone would ever measure up if I were to lose him.

"How is this possible?" Luke questions over my head, but I don't respond because I don't think he's talking to me. I believe he has the same internal war like me. So, I don't answer, but I understand. I've imagined, but I never actually thought that we'd be possible either.

Popular opinion says that Luke should be single. He's not supposed to have deep feelings for one woman, and he definitely shouldn't get attached. But I say screw everyone else's opinion. A connection like ours is hard to find and shouldn't be easily disregarded. We've got one chance at this, to prove *them* wrong. To take what we have and shape it into something that we believe in. Of course, I don't say any of that to Luke because it's not up to me. What we do together will have more of an effect on his life than mine.

I keep my ear to his chest, and instead of wondering how it's possible, I smile, grateful that it is.

Chapter Eleven

Luke

I never thought I'd use the D-word, but Rose and I have been dating for three weeks now. It still blows my mind how easily she's blended into my life. I still haven't told her about my brother, but I think that maybe it's time I do. We've gotten closer than I've ever been with any woman, and she deserves the truth from me and not to have it sprung on her by word of mouth. I'll tell her soon, but tonight we've got other business to attend to first.

The newlyweds finally came up for air after being back for a week and invited us over. The guys and I are going out to give Rose and Joselyn time to catch up without us lingering near.

I'm nervous because no one knows that Rose and I are official yet, except for Owen. He's the only one that I've told, and having that conversation with him was like speaking with my father. He'd already warned me about starting something up with Rose, but she's so damn irresistible. I doubt that anything Owen said, other than 'go for it,' the second time around, would have mattered. I was already in too deep.

"Are you ready for this?" Rose asks as we pull up to Dalton's house.

I put the car into park and turned my head to look at her. As nervous as I am, I've never been more ready. I reach across the armrest and grab her hand.

"Ready to show you off," I reply, winking at her.

Rose giggles. "I don't think this counts as a showoff. Everyone in there knows me," she gestures with her hand toward the house.

"But they haven't seen you with me." I bring her hand up to my lips and place a kiss on the back of it. "Trust me. You look different. Radiant. They probably won't even notice me with you at my side."

"Well, I'll notice you."

I lean closer to her. "We could skip out. I'm sure I can think of some excuse."

"So now you want to skip?"

I trace her bottom lip with my thumb. "That look you're giving me is changing my mind."

"I'm not giving you a look. And besides, they don't know about us, remember? So, what excuse could you possibly give them?" She laughs.

I'd forgotten about that small detail. I kiss Rose's hand again, groaning my frustration. "You're right." I let go of her hand and reached for the door latch. "Shall we?"

Rose and I walk up to the door together, and she rings the bell. It feels strange having to wait for someone to answer the door that I've freely walked in and out of before. Rose takes a noticeably deep breath, and I place my hand on her back, hoping to calm her. She looks at me and offers a small smile. Knowing that she's even the slightest bit nervous makes me that much stronger for her.

The door opens, and we both turn toward it.

"Look who finally decided to show up," Dalton says, focused on me, then his eyes move to Rose. He gives us a strange look, then peeps around us outside. "You two came together?" He asks as he steps aside, creating a gap for us to enter.

"Yeah. I thought Rose might need a designated driver tonight," I explained to Dalton. "Or I might need one," I say as we step inside, completely ignoring the confused look on his face.

The door closes behind us, and we walk further inside, moving toward the living room.

"So, you're friends now?" Dalton asks behind our backs.

I glance at Rose, chuckling under my breath. I know Dalton has questions. The last time he saw me, I could barely stand to be around her, or rather I tried to refrain from it thinking it was for the best. But things have changed. We're a lot more than friends now. *A lot more*, I think to myself. And my feelings for her are so strong that I want to give us a title, but titles make everything so complicated.

"Rose!" Joselyn seems to come out of nowhere, excitedly shouting Rose's name.

"Jos," Rose says, breaking away from my side. "I've missed you." They embrace each other like they've been removed for years instead of a few weeks. When they break apart, Rose grabs Joselyn's hand, spinning her slowly. "Turn around. Let me look at you." Joselyn completes her turn, giggling softly and holding her belly with her other hand. "You're glowing, mama," Rose tells her.

I find myself smiling at Rose for no reason at all other than seeing how happy she is. She's even more beautiful than the first time I saw her.

"I should say the same about you," Joselyn tells Rose, glancing my way and back at Rose.

"Wait," Dalton says, stepping around me, his eyes roaming between Rose and me. "Am I missing something here?"

I hear Owen's laughter coming from the kitchen. I wondered where he was when we stepped into the empty living room. He holds a bag of chips in one hand and a single chip in the other. "Good. The entertainment is finally here," he says. He walks past us, taking a seat in the chair that I used to sit in so that he can see everything. Then he tosses the chip into his mouth.

His actions would normally irritate me, but I'm not the least bit phased by him today. I shake my head at him and grin.

"Alright, what's going on?" Dalton asks.

I decide to put him and Joselyn, who's also staring at me now, out of their misery.

"Rose and I are together now."

"Together, together?" Dalton asks, his palms moving together and apart, then repeating, demonstrating his meaning.

"Are you clapping?" I ask him, chuckling. "Yeah. We're dating. Together," I add teasingly. "Are you guys ready to go?" I ask Dalton and Owen casually. "Pretty sure the ladies want to talk about me now."

"You're so full of it, Luke," Joselyn says, grinning at my comment. "And this may be the only time I agree with you."

Joselyn got used to my personality soon after we met, and over the years, she has gotten good at meeting me quip for quip. She's what I imagine a sister would be like if I had one.

"Yeah, let's go," Dalton says. "You're driving." He walks over to Joselyn and pulls her in for a kiss.

I mouth silently to Rose, "Come here," and she does. I can hear the crunch of Owen's chips in the background, but my eyes are focused on Rose and the sway of her hips as she approaches. I lean close to her ear, whispering, "We can't let them have all the fun." I wrap my arms around her, pulling her to me. Then I kiss her slowly, without hesitation, letting our friends know that this is where we stand. Rose's breath hitches before she gives in to me.

One second. Two. Five.

I ease away from Rose's lips, staring into her eyes. Her breath is shallow, skin blushed, eyes heated, and I don't want to leave her unsatisfied, but I must.

I brush my thumb across her cheek, smirking. "How's that for confirmation?"

Rose smiles. "Could've been better," she says teasingly.

"Well damn," Dalton's voice has us both looking his way. "I leave you alone for three weeks, and this is what happens?" He laughs.

Owen laughs. We all laugh, and an indescribable feeling takes over me. Not long ago, I wondered how the same two people could stand to be with each other day after day, but now I get it. I understand that look in their eyes, the subtle touches, their need to protect and care. I understand because I've found that with Rose. Every day that we spend together brings us closer, and every day that we're apart, all I want is to be with her.

Chapter Twelve

Rose

Joselyn and I watch the guys pull away through the front window. As soon as they're out of sight, we turn to face each other and let out a school girl scream. She throws her arms around me, and I hug her back. Joselyn has her guy. I'm the happiest I've ever been. I have Luke, and I'm going to be an aunt. It all calls for a celebration. A sober celebration.

We pull apart, and this time Joselyn twirls me. It feels good to behave like we did when we were teens and we had our first crush. It feels even better knowing that my first crush is possibly my last.

When the initial shock is over, we grab a bottle of water from the kitchen and sit down on the couch. I take a sip from my bottle and set it down on the end table, and Joselyn does the same. Only her sip is more like a gulp. I laugh, thinking how interesting it is watching her change, freely giving her heart, and sacrificing her body for someone that she can't see or hear yet. I wonder if I'll ever have that with Luke or anyone. I wonder if Luke even wants kids. If the thought of titles is a turnoff, then the idea of kids is most likely out of the question.

The thought of losing him—I swallow the pain of it. I can't think about that now. I have to stay in the moment. Otherwise, I'll drown.

"So," I say to Joselyn. "How was the honeymoon?" I ask, genuinely wanting to know but also trying to avoid the elephant in the room. I wasn't expecting Luke to show his affection for me in that way in front of everyone. I was just as surprised as they were, but I can't complain. If I had any doubts about how he feels, that move certainly took them away.

Joselyn smiles, and her eyes seem to shine with her thoughts. I wonder if I look as tranquil as her when I think about Luke.

"It was the best," Joselyn answers. "We took in a couple of sites, visited a couple of restaurants. Morning sickness kicked my ass a few times, giving Dalton a tiny taste of *'or worse.'* And we got plenty of practice for the next little one. I wouldn't change one thing about it."

"Sounds like you guys had a blast," I tell her. "And this place. Do you like the new look?"

"I do. Dalton's mom did a great job. It feels more like home, but I'm still looking forward to the new place, you know? Something that's truly ours."

"Will it be done before the baby comes?" I ask her.

"I should hope so. Otherwise, we need new builders. The little one isn't due for another six months," she grins, rubbing her belly. "That's more than enough time unless this one decides to come early." Joselyn squints her eyes at me. "You are deflecting, Rose. We've talked enough about me. It's your turn to spill." She kicks her feet up on the ottoman. "What the hell happened? That is not the same Luke we left behind."

"The ride home happened," I sigh. "I finally got sick of his attitude and asked him why he hated me so much and if he was afraid of me."

"You didn't," Joselyn covers her laugh with her hand.

"I did."

"Of course, you did. I don't know why I even asked." She rolls her eyes. "What did he say?"

"He said he didn't hate me, but he *was* afraid of his feelings." I shrug like his words did not affect me, but inside I can still feel what Luke breathing down my neck did to me at that moment.

"Luke said that?" She asks incredulously.

"Unbelievable, I know, but yes. He did. Shocked the hell out of me."

"So, how did you two end up in the same pod?"

"Well," I drag out. "I sort of invited him inside after the wedding. His confession led to more words, and before I knew it, I was asking him to stay the night, and we were waking up the next morning making a pact," I rambled, finishing with a deep sigh. "So, what the hell happened, you asked? Or should I say what is happening? I'm falling in love with him. Ugh," I groan, laying my head back on the couch, peering up at the ceiling. "I'm falling in love with him," I repeat softly as if the words are just registering, even though I've said them before.

"Wow," Joselyn says.

"Wow is right." I lift my head from the couch.

"This is a good thing, right?" She asks.

"Definitely a good thing. I just... I wish Luke had opened up more. He's talked about his parents a little but hasn't said a word about his brother. And I know we've only just begun, but the inquisitor in me wants to jump ahead. She wants to know what's eating at him."

Joselyn laughs.

"What?" I ask.

"You remind me of myself when Dalton and I were dating. They all have secrets Rose, and boy, did Dalton have a big one that I knew nothing about. But even when I didn't know what it was, I wanted to protect him somehow from that unknown thing. Just give it time," she says. "He'll come around."

"I see your motherly instincts are starting to kick in already. By the way, thanks for suggesting that Luke take me home. Best idea you've ever had."

I can honestly say that if Joselyn hadn't stepped in, Luke and I wouldn't be happening. He'd still see me as the

girl who broke his heart as a teen, and I'd still be wondering what I did to make him hate me.
"Did you expect something would happen between us?" I furrow my brows.
Joselyn shrugs, a sly smile appearing on her face. "I was hoping. I must say, though, I didn't think he'd be quite this receptive. You can be a handful."
"Hey," I protest, tossing a pillow at her and laughing as I do.
"*Well,* it's true, but so is Luke. I think you'll be good for each other. You've somehow managed to calm him down a bit, which is a feat in itself considering how much of a lady's man he is." The high I was on deflates at the reminder of who Luke is. Joselyn's eyes go wide as she covers her mouth for a moment. "Sorry, was," She corrects.
"But have I though?" I ask. "It's hard to say if he's changed. It's only been a few weeks. What's going to happen when he leaves again, and temptation is around every corner?" I know Luke has strong feelings for me, but are they strong enough for him to commit to only me?
"He'll have Dalton to keep him in line, and if he screws this up, he'll have to answer to me." Joselyn smiles, but I can't find it in me to join her.
"I'm serious. You remember what happened with him who shan't be named. And he wasn't even well known. There was no closure. He just left without an explanation, and it took months for me to bounce back from him. It'll take even longer if Luke were to..." I pause, not wanting to

finish that sentence. The thought of Luke not being in my life is hard to absorb.

"He won't," Joselyn tries to assure me. "Luke can be a lot of things, but one thing I know for sure is he's loyal. If he says that he's with you, trust that he is. Don't think about temptation because whether he's here or not, temptation is a constant. Focus on the vibe that he's giving *you*. Once you do that, everything else is just a blur in the background."

"I've missed you and our talks," I say, finally cracking a smile. "Though, I didn't expect I'd be on the receiving end again."

Joselyn adjusts her feet on the ottoman, using her hands to sit up straighter on the couch. I kick my shoes off and turn sideways with one leg bent in front of me.

"While I have you here, I want to run something by you," Joselyn gives me a mindful stare, one that tells me her next words are essential.

I grab my ankle, pulling my leg close to me. "What's on your mind?"

"William and I were discussing what's next for the podcast and who would be the face while I'm on maternity leave," she pauses. "Hope you don't mind, but I threw your name out there to see what he thought."

William is our boss, and he can be quite scary when he wants to be.

My eyes nearly bug out of their sockets. I've thought about joining Joselyn up on the tenth floor before. We've even joked about it, but I didn't know William would go for it with us being so close. Half of the time, I didn't think he liked me, to be honest.

"Mind?" I ask. "Why would I mind? I should be thanking you. What did William say?" I would love to have been a fly on the wall during that conversation. I fiddle with my hands and foot, impatiently waiting for an answer while Joselyn mocks me with her smile.

"Well," Joselyn draws out, continuing to torture me. She laughs, and I lift my foot off of the floor, softly kicking her propped calf. "Ouch," she complains, continuing her laughter.

"Oops," I shrug. "Now spill it."

"Well," she says again and pauses yet again.

"Well, what?"

"Starting Monday, you'll be shadowing me and hanging out behind the scenes to get a feel for what goes on. If you decide it's something you want to do, we'll bring you on, and you'll take over while I'm gone."

I bring the throw pillow up to my mouth and bite down, screaming into it. It's not until after my tongue touches it when I realize what I'm doing. I sure hope no one has had their feet on it.

"And," Joselyn continues. "When I come back, you'll be my co-anchor. That's if you want the promotion."

"So, does this mean I get a beautiful view too?" Before Joselyn got her position, she'd always wanted her office with a view, but she didn't think it was possible until it actually happened. I know I won't have the view she has.

I'm just teasing, but I'll have the next best thing. I get to work alongside her again, as we were before.

"You'll have a view of me if that counts," she jokes. "Your office would be across from mine."

I waved her comment away. "The view doesn't matter," I shrug. I'm just grateful for the offer. This is really happening. Now that I've been presented with a promotion, the thought is a little overwhelming, but it's nothing I can't handle. I smiled giddily at Joselyn. Then another thought occurs to me. "Tony is going to shit his pants. Does he know about this?"

"No one knows aside from William and us, but either way, Tony will be fine. After that stunt he pulled before, I doubt he wants to cause trouble. He's walking a very thin line since then. Besides, we need him where he is."

Tony is a co-worker that said some pretty inappropriate things to Joselyn at a work function years ago. He was angry because Joselyn got the job that he wanted. That ordeal almost got him fired. It also caused a snag in Joselyn & Dalton's relationship. If it weren't for Joselyn's generosity, he'd be on the streets. His talent is the only thing that saved him.

"I sure hope so," I say seriously. "Because if Tony tries to come after me, I won't be as nice."

Thoughts about my life and everything that's happening in it flood my mind. Everything seems to be flowing smoothly and falling in a straight line. It's almost too good to be true. Usually, when I get that feeling, something terrible is bound to happen.

Chapter Thirteen

Luke

I've managed to avoid the topic of my relationship with Rose for part of the ride to the restaurant. None of us were really in the mood to go to the bar, so we spent that time deciding on a destination. We settled on fast food and opted for a drive-thru and eating in a nearby parking lot to avoid drawing a crowd.

I can feel Dalton's eyes burning a hole through my head from the passenger seat. I imagine Owen's watching us both from the back seat and scrutinizing every move we make. Thankfully I'm driving, so I don't have to look at them. Owen already told me how he felt about Rose and me, but I haven't had that talk with Dalton yet. I can guess what he's thinking, though. His thoughts are probably similar to mine.

What the hell are you thinking?
You're a ladies' man.
Do you really think you can be with just one woman?
Don't drag her into your shit.
You don't deserve her.

I've thought about all of it and more, and yet, I can't seem to walk away from her. All of the reasons I should leave her alone are the same reasons that make me want to stay. For the first time in my life, I want to own up to my mistakes, and that's all because of Rose. She gets me like no one else ever has—not even the guys. I've only thought about being with her since we got together, and when it comes to my personal issues, she could probably deal with my shit better than I can. She's good for me. No, I don't deserve her, but I know that I need her.

I pull up to the drive-thru, press the down button for the window, and then place our order. I pull forward, coming to a stop at the main window, hoping to get through this without being recognized. The older lady at the first window seems irritated and doesn't crack a smile as she takes my card, swipes it, and returns it to me. I actually appreciate her irritation. It's nice not to be recognized. My appreciation is short-lived when I pull up to the second window. The young lady does a double-take and screams when realization dawns.

"OMG! It's you. DOL!" Her hands wave frantically in front of her, and I think she forgot she was at work. She looks around me and spots Dalton, then glances at the back window, but the tint is too dark for her to see inside.

I want to be rude, but I can't. So, I smile and say, "In the flesh."

She wipes her hand down her face to compose herself. Then she glances back into the restaurant and back at me, remembering where she is, I suppose.

"Your food will be right out, but," she pauses, looking back again. "Can I have your autograph?"

The guys are in the background laughing, and I'm about to say no when Owen winds his window down. "Sure, you can," he responds. "But can we make it quick because I'm kinda hungry," he teases, and she laughs.

She's in luck because Justin insists on us having something on hand just in case. I reach inside the armrest and grab one of our four by five cards with our picture on it and a marker. We sign it, and I hand it to her in exchange for our food. She thanks us profusely, and I pull away, thankful that we decided not to go inside. I love our fans, but at times I just want to be Lucas, the man.

A couple of minutes later, I park the SUV near the supermarket entrance, the furthest away from the store, while we eat.

"So, Rose, huh?" Dalton starts the conversation that I know he's been dying to have. I nod because what else can I say? "I kinda figured she'd be the one to turn you," he says, then takes a bite out of his burger.

"She's not a fucking vampire," I chuckle. But he's right. Rose has changed me. She's stirred a need in me that I didn't know I possessed.

"Are you sure about that?" Owen asks jokingly.

"Fuck you, Owen."

"I'm just saying," he continues. "Vampires can do some miraculous shit, and you're displaying all of the signs of someone under a spell."

"Laugh now," I tell Owen. "You're next."

"Hey. I'm not the one who's afraid of commitment. I'm just waiting for the right woman to come along and sweep me off of my feet."

"Aren't you supposed to be doing the sweeping?" Dalton asks, and we all laugh, continuing to eat our food. "And back to you," he eyes me closely. "Why now, after all these years?"

"I hadn't spent any time with her until now, which your wife practically forced me to do, by the way," I say pointedly. "I've always been attracted to her, but once we started talking… I don't know. She's different, and I feel something when I'm with her."

Dalton nods his understanding, and I know that he gets it. He's been where I am now. He's had similar feelings, if not the same.

"Do you love her?" Dalton asks, and my appetite for food disappears.

I've never been in love before, but I can say that I've never felt the way I feel for Rose about anyone else. I can say that I think about her as soon as my eyes slit open every morning. I can even say that she's my last thought before I fall asleep at night. When we're apart, I miss her like crazy, and when we're together, there's no place else I'd rather be. If that's love, then, "Yeah. I do."

"We should throw him a player retirement party," Owen suggests to Dalton. "Sorta like the bachelor party he threw you, to see if he's ready to throw in the towel."

"Are you hoping I fail?" I ask Owen.

"On the contrary, I want you to succeed. Rose is a good woman, and she deserves more than some guy who's going to dog her out."

My nose flares hearing him tell me what Rose deserves, but I keep quiet because it's the truth. I know what they think of me. I should have never allowed them to think I slept with all of those women. They never asked, so there was nothing to deny, which leaves me guilty by omission.

"I won't hurt her," I say more for myself than them. I began eating again, but it's more of a distraction than for sustenance. I barely taste anything. I have to get a grip. It can't be normal for one person to consume another this way.

An hour later, I'm picking Rose up from Dalton's and taking her home. Music filled the space during the ride. I stopped in front of her house and put the SUV in park, leaving the engine running. I reached for her hand over the console, needing the contact, and she laced her fingers through mine.

"I gather you're not coming inside," Rose says, glancing at the keys still in the ignition.

"I'm afraid not. Mom sent me a text earlier. Says she wants to talk." It's the truth, but also a lame excuse. I could go inside for a while, have my fill of her, and leave, but I wouldn't feel right about it. It would cheapen the experience.

Rose snorts out a laugh. "How cute," she teases. "You're blowing me off for your mother."

"I'm not blowing you off," I say, bringing her hand up to my lips. "I want you more than anything, but I need to deal with her first. Before we...," *can move forward*, I think, my words catching in my throat. I can't be what Rose needs until I get my life in order, which means I have to learn how to forgive in order to heal. "I've put it off long enough."

Rose pulls her hand from mine, raises the armrest, and slides over to my side. "Well," she says, straddling me. "If you're not coming inside, the least I can do is leave you with something to think about."

I raise an eyebrow. "Aren't you afraid of someone watching?"

Her eyes burn into mine, full of determination. "Not anymore."

Rose's fingers press into my shoulders as she kisses me, and I kiss her back slowly. Her tongue is warm, twisting with mine, and knowing that somewhere in the shadows, there are watchful eyes makes our actions even more intoxicating. Forbidden things always are. That's how every moment has been with Rose—thrilling because she's the one person that I shouldn't be allowed to have.

Rose grinds against me, the warmth of her center hardening me. I grip her jean-clad thighs wishing the material weren't between us. My hand slips beneath the shirt at her back, and her skin warms to my touch. I deepen our kiss as my hips buck against her. My dick throbs, begging to be inside of her.

Rose suddenly breaks away from my lips, her eyes closed and lips barely touching mine. Heavy puffs of air escape her lips as her breath presses and release against me in short spurts. I brush my nose to hers, nipping at her bottom lip with my teeth. I gently squeeze her ass.

"Fuck, Rose," I whisper, feeling so much in the moment. My soul hums for hers, and I know without a doubt that there is nothing I wouldn't do for her. "Truth for a truth," I say, moving my thumb across her cheek and over her ear. Rose opens her eyes, staring straight into mine, and she nods. "I'm falling in love with you too, Petals."

"And I'm afraid of this feeling," she adds.

"This is why I have to go. I don't want to cheapen this perfect moment." I place a simple kiss on her lips, lingering for a few seconds. Then Rose exits the truck on my side.

"See you tomorrow?" she asks.

"You will definitely see me tomorrow."

"Mom," I announce my arrival when I walk inside.

"In the living room," I hear her yell back.

Dad stands when I enter. "I'll let you two talk," he says, then walks over to mom and gives her a chaste kiss on her cheek. "See you in a bit, Kitty. Good night son."

The urge to vomit hits me, but I push the feeling back down. When dad leaves, I sit next to mom on the couch and prepare myself for an uncomfortable conversation. Mom gives me a solemn look, much like my own. I'm sorry that we have to have this talk too, but it's time.

"Son, I…"

"Mom, I…"

We start to speak at the same time and pause.

"You go first," She insists.

I blow out a long breath. "I'm sorry about the way that I've been acting for the past few years. I placed all of the blame on all of you for trying to fix my mistake when it wasn't entirely your fault. I could've stopped it at any time, but I didn't. You did what you thought was right, and I see that now, even if I disagree with it."

"I'm sorry too, son. I didn't realize what a mess we were creating at the time. We thought it was for the best. I'm your mother, Luke," she smiles sadly. "All I ever wanted to do is protect you."

"I know. I just couldn't accept it until now."

"And your brother. Will you ever forgive him?"

I don't know how to answer that. I want to forgive Jeremy. I know that I should, but… "I'm ready to talk with him," I answer the best way I know how and mom nods, a hopeful smile curving her lips.

"You seem happier," mom says, clasping her hands together on her lap. "Does your sudden change have anything to do with a certain young lady I've seen you photographed with?"

It has everything to do with her. I don't know if I feel comfortable having that conversation with my mother, though. I stare at her for a few seconds, wondering if I should let her in again. I trust her. I've never stopped trusting her, and she's not asking for much.

"She's had some influence," I say. "Her name is Rose." I can't help the smile that creeps on my face, and mom seems to be pleased. Her smile widens along with mine. I imagine all sorts of ideas running through her head, seeing my reaction to Rose's name alone. She knows my struggle and how hard it is for me to trust anyone.

"Well, I'm having a small get-together here next Saturday for the fourth. Maybe you could bring her with you."

"Maybe." I've never brought a girl home before for two reasons—one, I've never been in a relationship, and two, I consider that a serious step. One that I'm now willing to take, but I'll have to discuss it with Rose first. Meeting my family might spook her.

"Jeremy will be here too," Mom warns, her brows scrunching together.

I am ready to see my brother, but the mention of his name still causes my body to stiffen. "Good. Can't wait," I respond with a tight smile.

Chapter Fourteen

Rose

    I don't panic. I gather information, and analyze it then make a decision.
    I don't panic except for when it comes to Luke. He makes me overthink things, and that's what I've been doing since he asked me to accompany him to his parents for the fourth. Of course, I said yes because what else was I supposed to say. Luke is not the *take a girl home to meet his mom* type of guy. So, when he asked, I didn't think—I reacted, and now I can't stop thinking because of my reaction. This has to mean something, right? Or maybe not.
    "Ugh," I blow out a frustrated breath as I pace back and forth in my office. I didn't expect my first day of training to

be cloudy with a chance of disaster, but here I am, with a dark puff lurking over my head.

"Knock, knock."

I jump at the sound of Joselyn's cheerful voice, my hand lurching to my chest. "Jeez, Jos! You nearly scared the shit out of me," I whisper shout.

Joselyn completely ignores me, stepping just inside the door. "Are you ready?" She's all business as usual when she's at work.

"No. I mean, yes, but... Luke asked me to meet his mother," I blurt out.

"He...," Joselyn starts to speak then stops, closing the door from prying ears. "He did what?"

"You heard right, and I said yes, but now I'm freaking nervous." I plop down in my chair, and Joselyn eases into the chair in front of me. "I need someone to tell me that I'm doing the right thing—that we're not moving too fast."

"No one can decide that but you and Luke. Only you know how you feel and to what extent, and love can't be measured. It just is," She smiles. "In my experience, meeting someone's mother doesn't mean that he's proposing. It just means that he's serious about you. His attachment to you is great enough for him to share you with the other important people in his life."

I let her words soak in, and as they do, my tension begins to subside. I don't know if I like being on this side of the conversation. I guess I could have worse problems to worry about. This is an easy one, I think. I can do this. I try to convince myself that meeting Luke's mom is a small thing. It's the next step–a good step in the right direction.

"Your right," I tell Joselyn. I stand, smoothing my hand down my side. "I'm ready now."

Joselyn and I ride the elevator to the tenth floor and venture to William's office. His door is ajar, and his eyes focused on a stack of papers in front of him. Joselyn raps her knuckles on the door, and his eyes rise into his brows to look at us. He says, "Come in." His eyes return to his papers, then he adds, "have a seat."

Joselyn and I sit across from him, waiting for his full attention. He picks up a sheet of paper and places it in front of me.

"Rose Bush," William says. "Joselyn mentioned that you were interested in the open position." He stops talking, and his hard eyes focus on me.

Somehow, sitting in front of him now feels like we're meeting for the first time. I've been working here for years, have talked to him on occasion, yet this time, I feel like a stranger. A chill fills the air as he continues to stare. Then he raises a brow as if he'd asked me a question.

"Are you still interested?" William asks.

"Yes," I say a little too eagerly, fiddling with my hands on my lap. I close my eyes and take a moment to compose myself like the businesswoman that I am. *Breathe. He's only human*, I think to myself. I straighten my spine and look him square in his eyes. "Yes," I repeat. "I am."

"Good," he responds. "I assume Joselyn's already given you the rundown, so the only thing left to discuss is the salary, which I've detailed on the form in front of you. Take a few days to shadow Joselyn and look it over. Then, let me know what you decide by the end of the week."

I pick up the paper, skimming over the words until I find what I'm looking for. My breath catches at the printed figure. It's thousands more than what I make per year now, and I'd be a fool to turn it down. I swallow down my surprise, remaining in check. Then I stand, thank William and Joselyn for the offer, and let them know that I'll have a decision by the end of the week–even though my mind is already made up.

The sun is high in the sky when we arrive at Luke's parent's home on Saturday, and I'm as calm as a bird in a soft breeze. I've had nearly a week to process everything, and spending my free time with Luke has only made it easier. I'm prepared for whatever questions his parents may have and for all eyes to be on me. I'm even prepared to meet Luke's brother, who he finally mentioned in casual conversation. He still hasn't said what drew them apart, and I didn't try to pry it out of him. The important thing is he's letting me in. Every day he gives me a piece of him, and that's more than I'd ever expected.

Luke grabs my wrist, stopping me in front of his truck. "Truth for a truth," he says, joining our hands together.

"Sure," I answer, stepping closer to him.

"You are my strength," he confesses, placing a tender kiss on my forehead.

Luke's words pierce my heart like a thousand tiny needles all at once, and my eyes cloud over from the impact. Suddenly, him bringing me along means so much more than I even thought. This isn't about marriage at all. It's far more than that. This is about him needing me to ground him. It's about him doing this for himself and him doing this because of me. I don't know if I should be more afraid of the realization or ecstatic about it, but I do know that I love him with my whole heart.

"And you are my reason," I answer, tipping my head up to kiss him. It's a fleeting kiss, but it seems to promise the world.

"Mmm," Luke pulls away, his eyes holding mine. "You," he says, tightening and loosening his hands in mine.

"We should go inside," I suggest. "Your mom probably thinks I'm a harlot for making out in her driveway," I joke.

Luke chuckles, letting go of one of my hands, then we turn and start walking toward the house. He flicks the tip of my nose, then responds, "She knows there's only one type of woman I'd bring home to meet her."

"And what type is that exactly?"

"You," Luke answers with certainty.

I blush at his comment, and a warm, tingling sensation flows through me.

This man will be the end of me. I know it.

Luke uses his key to enter the house once we reach the front door. What he said and the realization of what's about to happen hits me again when we step inside.

I'm meeting his family.

My nerves try to get the best of me, but I taper them down, determined not to appear weak in front of his family. I suck in a deep breath then let it out.

"Are you okay?" Luke questions, placing his hand on my back.

"Yeah, I'm fine," I smile.

Luke watches me for a moment, then returns a smile. His hand remains firm on my back, unknowingly allowing me to draw the courage I need.

"My parents are harmless," he says as if he can read my mind. "Say the word at any time, and we can leave." His brows rise questioningly.

I nod my understanding, but I have no intention of leaving until he's done what he came to do. This is not about me. He needs this, and I'm here for him.

We step further inside, and Luke calls out, "Mom. We're here."

A few seconds later, a petite woman appears at the top of the stairs with a huge smile on her face. Her flowery sundress fans the base of her knees, and her eyes examine me as she descends the steps moving toward us. I feel like it's my first day of school, and I'm meeting a new teacher—only the feeling is multiplied by three. I want to make a good impression. I want to make the best impression. This is Luke's mom, and even if they aren't that close right now, her opinion matters to him—a mother's opinion always does.

"Rose," she says when she reaches us. Her delightful tone suggests that she's happy about me being here and takes away any reservations I may have had. "I'm Katherine, but you can call me Kat or Mom," she shrugs, glancing at Luke. "It's nice to meet you." She surprises me by pulling me in for a five-second hug. Her five-foot five frame is smaller than mine, but the weight of her arms around me makes her seem bigger somehow.

"Nice to meet you too," I say as she releases me.

She's a beautiful lady. I notice that Luke bears little resemblance to her except for their eyes. They have the same eyes, a little dark, a lot true. Her hair is light, while Luke's is dark. Judging by the way that she greeted me, their personalities aren't alike either. He must be more like his father.

"Come. Let's have a seat." She laces her arm through mine and guides me into the living room and onto the couch. Luke follows, taking the recliner next to us. "So, are you from around here, honey?"

"I am. Actually, Luke and I went to the same high school." I don't know why, but that seems to be an important fact. I don't want her to think I'm some *thing* he picked up while traveling.

"Really? I would love to hear all about how you two met."

"The first or the second time?" I ask her, and she glances at Luke.

"That's a story for another day," Luke chimed in, and a soft chuckle escapes me.

His mother, on the other hand, gives him a sad smile. It's clear she wants to know more—she said as much—but it's almost as if she's afraid she'll say the wrong thing. They're both so on edge. They obviously have a mother-son bond, but I can feel the tension between them. This thing that happened is definitely in the room, and it needs to be dealt with, or it will tear them completely apart.

Kat's shoulders lift and fall on a sigh. "Where are my manners?" She returns her attention to me. "The food isn't done yet. Dick's still outside on the patio tending the grill, but I can get you a drink if you'd like."

I nearly choke on my spit, and the frown on Luke's face doesn't help matters. I wonder what's going through that mind of his because my thoughts just took a wrong turn.

Kat pats me lightly on my back. "Are you alright?"

I nod, clearing the last of my blush from my throat. "Some water would be nice," I manage to get out.

Kat pats my leg then stands. "Be right back."

I watch Luke as his eyes follow his mother out of the room then over to me. "There's a lot more where that came from," he tells me with a hint of disgust in his voice.

"I'm sorry. I just... Dick? That's your father's name? I've never met a real Dick before."

Luke raises an eyebrow and chuckles while I die inside from embarrassment. My words are not playing nice today, and I pray that I can keep the bad ones confined to Luke's sole company.

"My father's name is William, but my mom insists on calling him that. Just wait until you hear her name. I think their mission was to torture us as kids, and they succeeded."

"Now you have to tell me." I widen my gaze at Luke, scooting to the edge of the couch, but he's not budging. Before I can tease it out of him, Kat returns with a bottle of water and hands it to me. "Thank you."

An Uncomfortable silence falls between us, and I wonder if this is how they've been behaving since Luke came home or if my presence is the culprit.

I take a few sips of water then replace the top on the bottle. "Your home is beautiful." It reminds me of my home growing up—the thick curtains, plush carpet, and the smell of fruit. I wonder if she's cooking a pie or if it's one of those trick air fresheners that my mom loves to burn.

"Thank you," Kat replies. "It could use an update. Time got away from us after the boys left, but it's still home, regardless of how dated it is," she smiles.

Luke's eyes move behind us, his expression turning dark. He grips the arms of the recliner so tight I think he might pull them off.

His mom turns around to follow his view and her smile falters. "Jeremy, you made it," she says, the excitement ripped from her voice. She looks trapped, so I can only imagine how she feels—like a thin red cloth between two raging bulls—like she has to choose. No mother should be put in that situation, but I'm not the one to judge because I have no clue what got them here.

The look on Luke's face, the lack of elation in his mom's voice, and the mention of his brother's name send a dirty chill through me that I wish I could wash off. I hate the rage in Luke's eyes, the tautness of his body, the way his jaw ticks at the person behind me. I don't like seeing him like this. I thought he hated me at first with the way he looked at me, but this is ten times worse.

Chapter Fifteen

Luke

Jeremy.

I hadn't even heard him come in.

I thought I'd prepared myself well enough for this moment, but that's the furthest thing from the truth. Seeing him brought everything rushing back—the love, the hate, the joy, the pain. Emotions are a bitch, and they're kicking my ass right now.

The same guy that was supposed to protect me turned out to be the one who hurt me the most. We made a promise when we were younger to never let anything come between us. I never thought that he would be the one to break it.

Jeremy was a smart kid and could weasel his way out of practically anything, which was probably a good thing considering he was always into something. I was always the smooth talker, but Jeremy, he was the fast talker–still is. He talked his way right into being a lawyer, but his heart was always too soft. I'll never understand how someone so smart could be so stupid. It's a terrible combination if you asked me, and if I hadn't known him so well, he would've had me believing the lie too.

I give myself a few seconds to calm down before loosening my grip on the arms of the chair. It took everything in me to not go over to Jeremy and punch him. I've never wanted to punish him more than I do now, but that's not what today is about. Today is about me moving forward so that I can be a better man for Rose.

I glanced at Rose for the first time since Jeremy entered the room. She's breathing just as fast as me, and her eyes are full of fear. I'm not sure if it's fear for me or what I might do, but it brings me back to what's important—back to her. My strength.

When I look at mom, her pained expression pleads with me to do this the right way.

I clear my throat, tapping my finger against the arm of the chair. "Mom, will you introduce Rose to dad please—give Jeremy and me a chance to talk?"

"Sure, son," she says, her voice a little shaky and far from sure. She stands, gesturing for Rose to stand with her. "Let's go so these two can hash out their differences."

Rose nods, but her eyes are still fixed on me when she mouths, "Are you okay?"

My feelings for her grow even more at that moment.

"I'm fine," I say for both her and my mother's sake. "I promise we'll leave the furniture intact," I try and lighten the mood while flashing a forced half-smile.

Rose finally stands and walks over to me, and I get the feeling she's not entirely convinced. She places her fingers in my palm with her thumb on top of my hand and squeezes lightly. "If you need me," she says with a concerned smile.

No other words need to be spoken. It's amazing how this beautiful woman has more faith in me than I have in myself.

I lift her hand to my lips then release it. "Thank you."

She and mom leave the room after taking a last glance at Jeremy. He's still in the same spot and hasn't said one word since his arrival. His hands are stuffed into his pant pockets as he stares at me. I can't decide if it's pride or fear or remorse in his eyes—or if it's a combination of all of them. Time seems to have slowed over the last few minutes. Maybe that's a good thing for Jeremy; that time gives me what I need to process this at my own pace.

If I were in his shoes, I wouldn't want to be the first one to speak. So, I do it for him.

"It's been a long time, *brother*," I spew out, not trying to hide the distaste in my voice. "Aren't you going to say hello? This is what you wanted, right? An audience with me?"

"Hey, Luke," he says, taking a few steps into the living room.

I look at Jeremy and realize that I know next to nothing about the man standing in front of me. I've spent so much time hating the big brother that I left behind. I didn't want to know the details of his life because then I'd have to forgive him. I wouldn't allow myself to condone his actions. I couldn't.

This stranger staring back at me looks like my brother, but he's different from what I remember—still smart as a whip because he knows not to get too close to me, but vulnerable and hesitant. His stance is everything a good lawyer shouldn't be.

"I'd say this is a good sign," Jeremy continues, coming to sit on the couch out of reaching distance. "You're here even though you knew I was coming."

"It's a sign that I can't live with this shit anymore. I have to let it go. So, yeah. I'm here."

"I've said it before, Luke, and I know you didn't want to hear it before, but I am sorry. There's no changing what happened. All we can do is move forward." Jeremy is quiet for a moment then, "I fucked up, Luke. I created a situation that I don't know how to recover from, but I have to try. I hurt my family. I ruined our happiness. I hurt you. If I had only done things differently, we would still be a family. I know that now more than anyone else. I miss my little brother."

Jeremy's sigh of remorse is felt from across the room. He braces himself, his elbows resting on his knees and head hung low.

I swallow down his unexpected apology. I guess I was expecting more of a fight, but he seems as if he's already defeated. I shouldn't, but I feel sorry for him. Pity is the last thing I expected to feel for Jeremy, but I can't show it. I won't let him off that easy.

"You're right. You did hurt me. You were supposed to protect me. Instead, you took away my want to find love and my ability to trust. You have no idea what it's like to carry that."

"I *was* trying to protect you."

I grin snidely, not entirely believing him. "Was it really me you were trying to protect or yourself? Have you ever asked yourself that question? Are you sure that you never once thought about your career—that a scandal would ruin your chances at a promotion?"

Jeremy opens his mouth then closes it.

"That's what I thought," I shake my head in disbelief, but I actually respect him for his silent admission. "You convinced me that brushing a crime under the rug and paying off some random female was the best thing for me."

"Your career had just begun, Luke. Something like that would've ruined you. Even though it wasn't true, it would've put a stain on you and your friends."

"She accused me of rape, Jeremy. Rape. And you paid the bitch off—far more than she deserved."

Jeremy flinches, his eyes flashing red for a moment. Somehow his reaction makes me happy—the fact that I fueled his brief stint of fire.

"I was only trying to protect this family," he says, this time including himself—and this time I believe him.

"I know you were, but it doesn't excuse what happened." *I can't keep dwelling on this. I have to let it go.* I remind myself mentally. I drop my eyes to the floor, drawing in a deep breath, then releasing it and looking back at him. "Look, Jeremy. You're my brother. Always will be. And because of that, I forgive you. I forgive myself for not standing up for me—for letting the wrong head guide me and for bringing that burden to this family. I'll never forget our mistakes, but I do believe there's a chance for us to behave like brothers again."

"I'm willing to try if you are," he replies.

"We're still a long way from sleepovers and camping trips, and there are some things I need to work through on my own, but yeah. I'm willing to try."

I feel like a weight has been lifted off of me. It's a start, but I know there's still a lot to work through.

"Can we continue this later?" I ask. "I've had enough talk about this for one day, and there's someone I'd like you to meet officially." I stand and walk over to Jeremy, and he stands in front of me. "There's just one thing I ask before you meet her."

"Anything," he replies with a nod.

"Regardless of what happens between her and me, any problems we may have, stay out of it. I'm a big boy now. I can fix my own shit, and if I can't, I know who to call for help," I offer a half-smile.

Jeremy cracks a smile for the first time since he got here. "I can do that."

"Good." I throw a fake punch to his arm, and he jumps. He should be grateful that's all I did. "Now, let's go eat."

Rose and mom are watching dad and laughing when Jeremy and I walk outside. I love hearing her laugh. I love seeing her getting along with my family. I'm not sure how she's going to react to Jeremy, and I shouldn't care if she likes him or not, but for some reason, I do. I'm angry at him, but I still love him regardless of everything we've been through.

Rose averts her eyes in my direction as we approach. I don't think I'll ever get enough of her beauty. I place my hand on her lower back when I reach her. Her laugh turns into a polite smile. She holds my stare for a moment, then glances at Jeremy and back at me, her eyes questioning. I plan to tell her everything once we're alone again.

"Looks like I'm missing all the fun. They're not filling your head with childhood stories, are they," I ask Rose.

"Not yet, but I can't wait to hear all about the trouble you've caused." Rose tweaks her eyebrow playfully, gaining a chuckle from me.

Being around her again calms me. I don't know what it is about her. I don't know where my head would be after my talk with Jeremy if I didn't have her to look forward to.

"Rose, this is my big brother Jeremy," I say, squeezing his shoulder between my fingers then letting go. "Jeremy, this is Rose—the woman I warned you about," I say pointedly, but only Jeremy and I know the true meaning of my statement.

"Warned?" Rose asks, and I shrug.

Jeremy nods, keeping his hands stuffed inside his pockets. "Pleased to meet you," he says.

"You too," Rose replies, a little hesitant, glancing at me.

I lean close to her ear, whispering, "I'll explain later," then kiss the side of her head.

I don't even understand my actions. One minute I feel as if I could kill Jeremy, and the next, we're standing next to each other like nothing ever happened. My mom and dad are watching me like I've grown a second head. Nothing about the way I'm behaving is normal for me. I don't kiss, hug, or bring girls home, and I certainly don't forgive easily. I kind of like the change in me. I have Rose to thank for that. I just hope she'll still see me the same when she finds out what I did.

After dad is finished, we eat while sitting around talking about random things. My parents learn a little about Rose, and they tell her what she wants to know, but no one dares breach any subject concerning me. I understand why my parents stay quiet, but not Rose. I had prepared myself for any questions Rose might have asked, but she didn't. She truly is the gift that keeps on giving.

Dad and Jeremy prepare the fireworks while mom stands by. I pull Rose away from them, needing a moment just for us. Fireworks used to be my favorite part of the fourth growing up, and I want to share one of my favorite things with Rose.

The sun is disappearing from the sky, making way for the darkness. I sit down on the bare grass and reach for Rose's hand. She takes it and sits between my legs, pressing her back against my chest. I like that she doesn't give a second thought to the grass possibly staining her jeans. She doesn't mind getting dirty with me.

"This is the best spot in the entire back yard," I tell her.

"Is that so?" she asks.

I glance over to make sure my family is still occupied. Then I pull her hair over her shoulder to her back. "It is now that you're here." I bend my neck to kiss her shoulder, then the side of her neck.

"Mmm," she lets out a soft moan, only quiet enough for my ears to hear. "Luke, your parents…"

"Are busy," I finish her sentence.

She turns her head to the side so she can see me, then bites at her bottom lip. I use my thumb to release her lip then replace my thumb with my mouth, kissing her slowly. Her body relaxes in my arms, and I don't want to pull away, but I do. I lean my forehead against hers, trying to calm the fire that I started inside of me.

"I've been waiting all evening to do that," I tell her.

"And was it to your satisfaction?" Rose bats her lashes, and I wish we were alone so I could take her right here.

I lick my lips—the taste of her still lingering there—as I continue to gaze into her eyes.

"Every moment that I spend with you, however momentary it may be, is satisfying, Petals. Every touch," I say, pressing my palm to Rose's belly, pulling her closer. "And every breath." I trail my nose down the side of her face. Rose gasps as my breath trickles over her skin. "And every kiss." I place a simple kiss on her lips, and she closes her eyes briefly, letting it sink in.

When Rose opens her eyes, she looks away from me without responding. She sighs heavily, and I wonder what brought on the sudden change. We sit in the same position, with Rose leaning back against me and my arms around her, in silence until dad announces that his firework show is about to begin. Then I lay back in the grass, taking Rose with me. She rests her head on my shoulder, nestling into the open space at my side as she gazes up at the dim sky.

The sky lights up in a burst of color, one after the other, reminding me of the way things used to be. I turn my gaze away from it to watch Rose's reaction. I had expected to see a smile on her face, but her expression is deliberate, like she's thinking about so much all at once.

Rose reaches up for my hand that's draped over her shoulder and entwines our fingers together. "Thank you for giving me this," she says without looking my way. "Is this what it was like growing up here?" she asks.

I open my mouth to answer her, but before I can, a childlike scream erupts behind us, shouting, "Daddy!"

What the fuck?

I freeze at the small voice. I knew Jeremy had a child, but I've never met him. I don't even know the kid's name because I let our issues get in the way of what was important—family. Me seeing the kid probably wouldn't have changed, but I could've at least learned his name.

Rose turns her head in my direction. Then she sits up to get a better look. "Luke," she says.

I sit up and look at Rose. A dreadful feeling fills me, my body heating from head to toe. I stand and reach for Rose's hand, and she grabs hold of mine, standing with me. I shouldn't have brought her here.

"Luke," she says again, but I'm speechless.

I turn toward the house. Jeremy is holding his son now, and the kid is smooshing his dad's face between his tiny hands. I want to be happy for him because he seems to have a tight bond with the kid, but I can't.

If Jeremy's kid is here, then his mother is not far behind.

"Rose," I finally speak. "We need to leave *now*."

"What's going on?" she asks.

This isn't how I wanted her to find out. "I'll explain later, okay?" I don't want to make a scene. I just want to go.

I guide Rose toward the house where my parents are standing, so we can say goodbye. There's no way I'm coming back here tonight. Jeremy and I smoothed things over as much as possible with our relationship, but this is another monster entirely.

"Mom. Dad. We're going to take off. I won't be back tonight."

They both nod, then mom's head turns toward the back door. I hold Rose's hand like a lifeline, determined not to let go because I'm afraid of what I'll do. I follow mom's gaze and come face to face with Marcia—Jeremy's wife, and the woman that accused me of rape. Her eyes scan over me, and she smiles as if nothing is wrong—as if this situation is normal. My chest heaves with rage, eager to be released. My skin pricks with disgust when she drawls, "Hi Luke."

I feel sorry for my brother, who's stuck in a loveless marriage, and for his innocent child, who has no clue how devious his mother is.

I ignore Marcia, turning away and taking deep breaths, still clinging to Rose's hand. Without another word, I walk away, taking Rose with me.

Chapter Sixteen

Rose

I want to help Luke, but I don't know how or what I'd even be helping with. Everything happened so fast, and he's been distant ever since. The car ride home was ice cold, and now we're sitting outside my house in silence. I have so many questions that I'm afraid to ask.

What happened between you and your brother?
Why did we have to leave so suddenly?
Who was that woman?
Are you okay?
Are we okay?

I'd like to think that whatever he's holding inside can't be that bad, but something tells me it's far worse than I imagined.

Luke has been throwing up red flags since the day we came face to face again. Maybe I should've heeded his warning, but then I wouldn't have gotten to know him. Now I have to decide if this fight for love is worth it—if this thing between us is strong enough to withstand what lies ahead.

I thought I had learned my lesson about getting attached to people, but obviously, I haven't because here I am. My heart is attached, and I can't just quit Luke. He's not the type of person you just walk away from—not unscathed at least. He's the type to break hearts without even realizing it, and my heart would definitely break if I were to lose him. I can feel the bruise just thinking about it.

I open my mouth to speak, but the only thing that comes out is a gasp of air. A lot has happened today that I'm clueless about. Luke is feeling the effects, which means I can feel it too. Heat and anger radiate off of him, and he's in no shape to go back home. He knew it before we left.

I'm afraid of what he might do if I let him leave here alone.

"Stay with me," I say, turning my head in his direction.

Luke closes his eyes and lets his head fall back onto the headrest. His eyes open, and he stares at the roof of the car as if he's contemplating something. I notice he does that a lot around me, and I don't know what to make of it.

He doesn't look at me when he says, "I can't ask you to do that, Rose."

"You didn't," I say, letting the reality of my statement sink in. "Stay with me," I say again. "For as long as you need to."

"What are you saying, Rose?" Luke asks.

I realize my statement sounds like a proposal, but that wasn't my intention.

"I'm not proposing any more than what we already are," I say quickly. "You can take the spare bedroom. I just want you to be safe." *And not do anything stupid.*

Luke finally looks at me, and amidst the pain evident in his expression, there's also curiosity. His stare is so intense that it warms me to my core. It's as if he's searching for answers. His voice is strained when he says, "Okay." He pauses, his eyes still searching, then adds, "But I need to ask you something first, and I need you to be honest with me."

My heart.

This man.

It doesn't matter what his question is. "Honest is all I'll ever be with you."

"Do you trust me?" He asks, and I want to remind him to breathe because it doesn't look like he is.

So much that it scares me, I think to myself. "I do." I trust him with everything that matters.

He releases a long breath.

"Can we make tonight about us?" He asks. "I just want to hold you."

I wish he would stop talking, and not because I don't want to hear his voice, but because his words are scaring me. Every word feels like a chip at what we are, and I fear that this night might be our last.

Regardless I answer, "Whatever you need," because those words feel like the right thing to say.

We strip down to our underwear and climb into my bed once we're inside the house. Luke stays true to his word. He pulls my back flush against his chest, and we spoon. He wraps me in his arms and holds me. Neither one of us says a word. I feel like this is one of our more defining moments.

We lay like that for over an hour with his breath tickling my skin and his hand rotating between my belly and my thigh. I fight against the weight of my eyelids until Luke's breathing becomes heavy. Then I succumb to sleep too.

I stir in my bed, reaching my hand behind me to the other side only to find it empty. My eyes pop open as the memory of yesterday comes flooding back to me. I'm reluctant to turn around out of fear that Luke may be gone. Then I hear it—the sound of a throat clearing behind me. I turn over onto my side. Luke is sitting in the only chair in the room with his gaze fixed on me. He's smiling, but it's not full. It's weak and melancholy, and the fire that usually burns in his eyes is gone. He seems defeated, and I feel helpless. I don't even know what to say to him. So, I stare back at him, waiting for him to decide how this plays out.

"Good morning," Luke finally drawls out with fatigue lining his voice.

"Morning," I respond with a smile. I glance at the alarm clock on my nightstand. "You're up early."

Luke looks down at his lap, his fingers fiddling with something I can't see on his bare leg. "Couldn't sleep," he says with a shrug, then moves his eyes back to me.

It's probably wrong for me to notice how good he looks sitting in my chair, but I do. I can't help it. He's a magnet, and everything about him is inviting—as I said before—a red flag. He's not perfect by any means. His skin doesn't glisten like it does on the television and in print, but his muscles are tight. His hair is disheveled, and he has more worries than most, but that's what makes him so perfect for me. He doesn't claim to be someone he's not when he's with me.

I clear my throat, pushing those thoughts to the back of my mind, and sit up, holding the sheet over my chest like he hasn't seen me half naked before.

"Is it something I can help with?" I ask seriously. He needs to vent before he explodes. I know it, and he knows it. Though, I understand his hesitancy. We've only been dating for a few weeks, and I'm assuming his issues stem from a lack of trust. He has to know by now that he can trust me.

Trust is a two-way street. So, I return his words to him. "Do you trust me, Luke?"

He eyes me carefully. "Of course, I do. That's why it's so hard for me to say what I have to say. I don't want to lose you, Rose." His pained expression is hard to bear, but I swallow it down anyway.

"Are you breaking things off with me?" I ask.

Luke knits his brows together in concern. "That's the last thing that I want, but you might want to be rid of me after you hear the whole story."

I adjust the pillow behind me so that I can sit up straighter on the bed. I clutch the sheet tighter within my grip, needing something tangible to hold on to.

"Tell me," I say, looking Luke straight in his eyes while bracing myself for the worst.

Chapter Seventeen

Luke

Where do I begin?

I barely slept last night. Even in my dreams, I couldn't seem to escape the chaos that's my life. I woke up to Rose's ass pressed against me in the middle of the night. She was sleeping so peacefully, and I didn't want to wake her. So, I got out of bed and claimed a spot in the chair. I've been staring at her ever since—not in a creepy way. I just couldn't stop wondering if she's the forgiving type—if her feelings for me will continue to blossom once she knows the truth.

"A few months after the band started touring, I literally ran into trouble," I begin, and I have to look away from Rose to continue. I avert my eyes to the wall on the other side of the room. Every single detail from my past is fresh on my mind as if it happened moments ago. "I was young and naive, and I know that's no excuse, but I wasn't prepared for life in the fast lane. I didn't know how cruel people could be. Being introduced to so much all at once, I felt invincible, and I behaved as such."

I pause to glance at Rose, and she's clutching her sheet so tight. I hate seeing the fear in her eyes, and I want to go to her, but I can't.

"One night after one of our shows, I ran into this girl. She seemed innocent enough at the time. We ended up in a hotel room alone, and I had sex with her. It was nothing I hadn't done before, but for some reason, I thought I could trust her to be like the other four. I thought she'd disappear from my life, and I'd never see her again, but that's not what happened. The morning after, she'd taken polaroids of us lying in bed together. I was asleep, and she was next to me, but she had bruises on her neck and arms—her proof that I had choked her and held her down. She claimed that I forced her to do it."

Rose gasps, her eyes widening in dismay. I feel nauseous and frightened that I'm going to lose her, but I continue.

"I promise you, Rose, that I didn't do it. I would never force myself on anyone. I was so angry at her and myself because I knew I'd fucked up. I also knew that her lies could mean the end of a career that I had just started, but I didn't care. We argued about it, but nothing I said would change her mind. She told me she would go to the press if I didn't give her ten thousand dollars. I didn't have that kind of money to give away, and even if I did, I refused to be blackmailed. She gave me forty-eight hours to decide and left."

Rose sighs, and it's hard to know what she's thinking. Her grip on the sheet isn't as taut now, which I take as a good sign. So, I continue.

"Of course, I had to tell the guys because my decision would affect all of us."

A sorrow-filled breath leaves me as I think about what telling them was like. They were so supportive and told me they were with me regardless of what I decided. They even offered to pitch in money if I decided to pay her off.

"I told our manager, Justin, next, and then we flew home so that I could tell my family in person. I'll never forget that day—all of us in one room deciding my fate. I wanted to fight her accusation. She had already taken my trust. I didn't want to lose my dignity too, but Justin and my family convinced me that a payoff would be the easiest option and less time-consuming. They said it was best for everyone—less money spent—far less than what she asked if we went to court. Jeremy was fresh out of law school, and he'd just landed a new job. He didn't want his name tied to a scandal. So, he took care of everything. We got the money, and he paid her in cash. I was ashamed of what I'd let happen and even more ashamed of the relief I felt at never having to see her face again."

I pause to gauge Rose's reaction. There's not an ounce of judgment in her expression. She just watched me with keen eyes, and I stare back at her.

"My relief was short-lived," I continue. "I found out after the fact that a few days after Jeremy paid her, she contacted him again with another demand for more money. Jeremy was smart. He'd destroyed the photos the first time around, but she was smarter. She'd recorded a conversation they had with some incriminating details. Her actions made me believe that we weren't her first targets. Jeremy," I say, dropping my eyes to the floor and shaking my head in disbelief. "I assume he knew that his career would be ruined if that recording ever got out. So, he made her a counteroffer—one she didn't refuse. He ruined his life to save his career and mine by marrying her. If I had known what he was planning," I pause, my heart breaking all over again.

The sound of skin brushing against fabric reaches my ears, but I keep my head hung toward the floor. Rose's bare feet cover my vision, and her fingers touch the space below my chin, pulling my head up to meet her eyes. She's so beautiful, and she's still here. I'm so lucky to have her.

"There was nothing you could do," she says in the sweetest, most sincere voice.

"I could have tried to talk him out of making the biggest mistake of his life," I responded.

"You could have," Rose says, stepping between my legs. "But from what you've told me about your brother, he wouldn't have listened."

Rose is right, but if I had tried, I would at least have a clear conscience.

"How are you still here?" I ask Rose. "How could you still want me?"

A smile graced her lips as she gazes into my eyes. It's as if she remembers something.

"We all have a past, Luke. I can't fault you for yours any more than you could fault me for mine. Everything that happened brought you back to me, and I can't be mad at that. You are not that young, naive boy anymore," she says, craning her neck to kiss my forehead then pull away, her eyes returning to mine. "You are not responsible for your brother's actions. He did what he did for his reasons alone. He made a choice, and he's living with it. Now you have to find a way to live with yours."

I touch my forehead to Rose's chilled belly and wrap my arms around her, pulling her closer. Her words seep into my skin as I think them over. I've forgiven my parents and Jeremy, but I still carry a burden because I haven't forgiven Marcia. I have to find a way to forgive her, too, because whether I like it or not, she's not going anywhere. She's married to my brother, and she's my nephew's mother—two facts that can't be erased.

I tilt my head up and place a kiss at the space right below Rose's sunken belly button. It's not lost to me that if I dip my head a few inches further, I could taste her. I could drown myself in her and forget about everything for a little while, but it wouldn't last. As soon as it's over, I'd be drenched in sorrow and confusion again. As appealing as the thought is, I won't do that to her. Not like this.

I grip Rose's hips, and she moves back a few inches, widening her legs and straddling me. She doesn't know how hard it is for me to resist her, with less than an inch of fabric separating us. The slightest movement of her hips, her warmth brushing against my morning wood, has me gripping her waist tighter.

Rose cups my face in her palms then leans in for a kiss. She pulls away, covering her mouth with her hand as she says, "Sorry."

I chuckle. "Morning breath is the last thing on my mind," I tell her while reaching around to squeeze her ass. "You make it so hard for me, Petals," I say, pun intended.

"I could walk away," Rose teases, attempting to stand.

My heart leaps forward unexpectedly, and I pull her back onto my lap. I know she was only kidding, but I still felt the urge to hold onto her. I need her more than I realized. I kiss her shoulder then pull back to look into her eyes. Her playful smile falters as she holds my stare, recognizing the seriousness of this moment.

"Truth for a truth?" I ask.

Rose wraps her arms around my neck and nods.

"I don't want to do this without you." I swallow, closing my eyes, letting my truth sink in. I've been doing that a lot with Rose—experiencing many new feelings—wanting to do meaningful things. I want my life to mean more than beats on a drum. I want to be more than someone's pawn, or son, or brother, or friend. I want to pour everything that I am into one person, giving myself completely. I know now that person for me is Rose. I just hope she feels like I'm that person for her. I need her to trust me with the sum of her too.

When I open my eyes, Rose is still staring at me with her truth evident in her misty eyes.

"You won't have to," she says in a low, raspy voice. She places a steady kiss on my lips, sealing her promise, then touches her forehead to mine.

Rose and I showered, then spent the rest of the morning cuddling in bed naked. I had a valid excuse. Since I left my parent's home in a rush last night, I didn't have a change of underwear. Rose figured she'd join me, stating that she didn't want me to feel like an oddball. It was nice lying next to her that way without acting out my feelings—not that she didn't try to tempt me. My feelings from earlier haven't changed. The next time I'm inside her, I want every thought to be about her. I want my past to be sorted.

Now I'm sitting at the bar commando-style beneath my jeans while Rose makes us a nut-berry sandwich for lunch. If she were to bend over, I'd be able to see her cheeks under her shorts. It seems she's hell-bent on torturing me.

She turns around and sets a plate in front of me. "For you," she says, then grabs her plate and sits next to me.

"So, what's going on with you?" I ask, needing to focus on something else. "How's the shadowing going?" I take a bite out of my sandwich, waiting for her answer. We've spent the entire weekend concentrating on me. I need a reprieve, and I genuinely want to know about her. She'd mentioned that she was up for promotion earlier this week, and I wanted to do something nice for her to celebrate, but that was before things went horribly wrong yesterday.

A smile creeps onto her face, and she glances at me. "I think I'm going to love it. Joselyn has been great, and William," she pauses. "Well, he's still William. I think I'm growing on him, though." She breaks off a corner of her sandwich and pops it into her mouth.

I love how passionate she is about her work—that she has this thing of her own to keep her company when I go back on tour.

The screen on my phone lights up, signaling a message from Jeremy, and I ignore it. "So, when should I expect to see your beautiful face in lights?"

I've been ignoring all of my messages since last night—not just the ones from Jeremy, but also the ones from mom. I wasn't ready to know what they had to say, and I needed today with Rose so she'd know what she's getting herself into.

Rose glances at the screen, then at me, as if my question doesn't matter. "Aren't you going to see what he wants?" She asks.

"I will. Soon. I just…" I pause, thinking about it. Having an open wound for years of my life hurt like hell. Just when I thought I was on the verge of healing, I came face to face with the source of that pain, and the wound was ripped open again. A wound like that—to be sliced open in the same spot—is even harder to heal the second time around.

Rose puts her sandwich down and grabs my hand.

"I used to wonder what it would be like to have a sister or a brother growing up. I mean, my life was great, but the unknown was always there nagging me. You don't have to wonder, Luke, because you have it. Yeah, it may be a lot chaotic at the moment, but he's trying, and I know you want to try too. Otherwise, it wouldn't hurt so much."

Rose lets go of my hand and goes back to eating her sandwich. She's right. She's like the female version of Owen, citing profound shit—as he likes to point out.

"Soon," I reply as the phone lights up again—and I ignore it again.

Chapter Eighteen

Luke

I stopped by my parent's house a few days ago to pick up my things while they were out. I decided to take Rose up on her offer to take her guest bedroom. I even offered to pay her, but she wasn't having it. So, my clothes have their own room now because I haven't slept in it one night since I've been there.

After three days, I finally answered Jeremy's text on Wednesday, telling him that I'd meet him at our parent's later this evening. Though, I have to meet with the guys at Dalton's first. It's been weeks since we've rehearsed, and I think we all miss it. I know I do.

I love our fans. I love the life that they've afforded me. I love traveling and experiencing different things, but that's not what I miss the most. The music is what I miss. It's a part of me—the way it seems to seep into my skin and speak to my soul. When I'm pounding away on my drums, I'm found. I'm at peace. I let the rhythm sway me, much like Rose does. I think it's why I'm so attracted to her. She reminds me of music.

Rose has been so good for me, but when she's at work, and I have nothing but time, my mind goes haywire. I need something to occupy my days. I even considered asking my dad if he needed any help at the site. When Dalton called, it's like my prayers had been answered.

Dalton and Owen are set up in the garage when I arrive. I guess we lost our spot in the living room when Joselyn moved in. We exchange greetings and jump straight into practice. It's as if we'd never skipped a beat. We all play our roles to near perfection. I needed it. I think they did too. We play for three hours straight with few stops in between to tweak some things. Afterward, I wash the sweat from my face and join the guys in the kitchen for a snack.

It's quiet for a long while, reminding me of our custom after every performance—only today, we don't have to entertain fans afterward. They have no idea what's happened with me over the past few days, but somehow, I feel as if I'm wearing the truth on my sleeves, and they're waiting for an explanation.

"So, I saw Jeremy over the weekend," I say offhandedly.

Both of them turn to look at me with shocked expressions.

"How did that go?" Dalton asked after a few seconds had passed while Owen did his staring thing as if he already knew the answer.

I gulp down a drink of water and sit the bottle down on the table, circling it between my fingers.

"Before or after Marcia showed up?" I ask, raising an eyebrow.

"Whew," Dalton responds.

"Whew is right. Everything was going as well as could be expected. Jeremy and I talked and agreed that we'd be…" I paused, thinking of the right word to use when you're occasionally in someone's presence, but you don't want to be—the way I used to feel about Rose. "Cordial," I finish, throwing a pointed glance Dalton's way—using the same word he used.

"The fireworks had barely begun, and then a bomb came crashing in and ruined the whole evening. If Rose hadn't been there…"

"Rose was there?" Dalton asks as Owen's brows rise.

"Yeah, she was, and she may have saved Marcia's life," I reply. "I'll never understand why Jeremy married her."

"You said you guys made up, right? You and Jeremy?" Dalton asks, and I nod. "So, what are you going to do about Marcia?"

"I don't like it, but I have to forgive her, for myself and Rose's sake."

Owen looks impressed by my answer. "Know what we need?" he finally chimes in.

I pinch my brow together, tilting my head a little. "To be rid of Marcia?" I guess.

Owen chuckles. "That's what you need. I think a show would do us all some good. Nothing huge. Maybe a week away or an overnight performance," he suggests.

I shrug. I wouldn't mind it. In fact, I'm sure I'll welcome it after meeting with Jeremy later this evening.

"Set it up, and I'm there," I say, looking to Dalton for a response.

"I'm all for it. Of course, I'd need to run it by Josie first. I'm sure she wouldn't mind. I just don't want to be away from her for longer than a week with the baby coming."

I hold back a laugh at the fact that Dalton has to ask permission to do his job.

Dalton looks at me and lets out a low chuckle. "Give it time," he says as if he's read my mind.

The smile disappears from my face once my reality dawns—how things are about to change for me. If Rose and I continue on the path we're on, and we were to marry, I'd be reciting those same lines.

"I think he's finally got it, Owen," Dalton says smugly. "Josie knew the kind of life she was signing on for, Luke. She knew that I'd be away for weeks, sometimes months at a time. Me consulting with her is not about her telling me what to do. It's about love and trust. It's about me respecting her enough to make decisions together and her doing the same for me. Remember that."

My eyes float to Owen and back to Dalton, wondering if this is what life will be like from now on—them continually giving me advice. It's good advice, but it makes me feel like an older man. I'm quickly turning into Lucas, the real man, but I think I'm okay with that. Rose is worth it.

"I know at least one other person who will be happy," Dalton says, reverting to the topic. "Justin wasn't exactly ecstatic when we told him we were taking so many months off."

"He probably has something on standby already, just in case," I agree. "You know his motto."

"You have to stay relevant," We all say together, then laugh.

Dalton makes the call to Justin with Owen and me listening in on speakerphone. As I had suspected, Justin had something on standby, more than a few things. He told us that there's an opportunity on Friday night—a last-minute cancellation if we were feeling up to it. It's a day drive away, and we'd be gone for three days tops. After that, he could set us up for one performance per month until the new year, if we agreed to it. They would all be day drives except for one, and no longer than a week away from home. We told him we'd let him know something tonight, and he ended the call with his famous line—*You have to stay relevant*—which earned a full-blown laugh from us.

Jeremy's car is in the driveway when I arrive at my parent's home. Before I can get the truck into park, a drizzle begins, coating my window with tiny droplets of rain. I can't decide if that's a good or a bad sign. Maybe it's God's way of telling me I should leave while I can. Or him warning me that an even greater storm is coming.

I gaze through the window and up at the dark grey clouds. Only minutes ago, the sky was clear, and things seemed promising, but now I'm not so sure. The rain shows no signs of slowing down, and the droplets become thicker and more frequent the longer I sit here.

I get out of my truck and jog to the front door, not wanting to get completely soaked. I drag my feet across the mat before opening the door and stepping inside. It's eerily quiet when I enter, unusually so. As I get closer to the living room, I can hear voices whispering. When I turn the corner, three sets of eyes land on me. Mom, Dad, and Jeremy are spaced around the living room in a gloomy semi-circle that feels like an intervention setup. I stop, eyeing them all carefully.

"Have a seat, Luke," my father says.

Mom gives me a look of sorrow, while Jeremy seems nervous.

Questions run rampant through my mind. What reason would Jeremy have to be nervous? Why does he want to talk to me? What does this have to do with my parents?

I can't seem to turn off the thoughts, and I still haven't moved from my spot.

"Luke," Mom says this time, and my eyes cut to her. "Please sit down, son."

"What is this?" I ask, finally able to form words.

"Luke, please," Jeremy begs.

I step further inside, relenting to their plea. I sit in the unoccupied seat that was clearly left for me. It's the furthest away from the exit, making any attempt to flee difficult. I look at Jeremy, calm as a breeze but still cautious, and ask, "Why am I really here?"

He presses his back to the couch as one hand grips the arm. "We need to talk," he says as if that's a clear answer.

"Look, if this is about you and me, we're good. There's nothing left to say." My heartbeat picks up speed. Something about this whole thing doesn't feel right—it hasn't since the moment I pulled up out front.

"This is beyond me and you," he replies, turning his head toward the entrance. As if on cue, Marcia appears looking every bit as flustered as Jeremy.

"What the fuck, Jeremy?" I say without regard to my parents. Now I'm the one gripping the arm of my chair. I can't think straight. I feel trapped in their circle of deceit and mistrust. There's only one way out, and Marcia's blocking it. My blood begins to boil, my mind racing along with it, and this time I don't have Rose's hand to ground me. I close my eyes and think of her, my strength. I drown them out and count to sixty. When I open my eyes, Marcia is sitting next to Jeremy on the couch. I stare at them, trying to hold back the malice I feel.

Isn't this what I wanted? For us to be in the same room and not kill each other? Granted, I didn't expect it tonight, but we're here. There's no stopping it now.

"Talk," I demand, ready to be done with this.

"Marci," Jeremy says to his wife, then takes her hand in his.

I tilt my head slightly, examining their actions. They appear to be closer than I thought—behaving like a real couple. I look down at their joined hands, then back to their faces. Marcia leans closer to Jeremy, and he allows it.

"It's okay," he assures her, giving her hand a gentle squeeze.

All this time, I thought that their marriage was a business arrangement, but it seems that's not the case.

"What's going on here?" I ask, giving everyone in the room equal eye contact. I stay quiet, waiting for some type of explanation for what I'm witnessing.

"Luke, try to stay calm and keep an open mind," mom says pleadingly. "She only wants to make amends."

Nothing good ever comes after words like that.

I look at Marcia, my nose flaring, and move my hand for her to speak. She clears her throat, her eyes still dark but not in a malicious way. They house a hint of sadness and maybe even regret.

"I'm sorry, Luke, for everything that I've done to hurt you," she says. "I know it doesn't mean much, but I am so sorry," she repeats.

"If you know how much it means, then why bother saying it?" I ask.

Marcia flinches as if I'd hurt her feelings. The sassy, unapologetic girl I met years ago is gone. She answers my question with a shrug.

"What I did to you was wrong," she says, pausing. "What I did to Jeremy was even worse." She glances at Jeremy and back at me. "I didn't deserve it, but he forgave me, and we fell in love."

I chuckle maniacally, not believing my ears. "This is a joke, right, Jeremy?"

"It's true," he answers. "Our marriage started as a sham, but things changed. We've changed, and we're having a baby."

I need some fresh air. I move to stand, but my mother stops me.

"Son, please sit down. Hear them out. This has gone on long enough," she says.

I reclaim my position; my eyes fixed on them again. *What am I missing? He can't be serious.*

"Luke, the night that you and I, uhm…" Marcia glances at Jeremy, and he nods for her to continue. "Jasper is our son, Luke," she says, her hand moving from me to her. "We have a son."

What the fuck?

I can't breathe, and my vision blurs. It feels like my heart is collapsing in on itself. Of all things, I never would've imagined this—and from my brother no less.

I have a son who thinks that my brother is his father.

Without thinking, I stand, grab the lamp off the table, and smash it to the floor. Then I feel my feet moving. I hear shuffling behind me, but I don't stop. I can't. I hear my mother's voice say behind me, "let him go alone." One set of footsteps follow after me, but I continue. I open the front door and continue down the steps and into the pouring rain. I bend over; my hands braced on my knees. I feel the urge to hurl, but nothing comes out but dry air. My legs weaken, and I fall to my knees in the grass, my head hung toward the ground. Everything hurts, but I don't feel a thing.

"Luke." I hear Jeremy's voice through the rain. "Come back inside," he says, but I can't move. So, he kneels next to me.

I feel like such a fool. What do I do now? How do we move on from this? I tilt my head up to the sky and barely breathe out, "Why?"

Jeremy stands after a few minutes, and I feel his hands moving beneath my arms from behind, lifting me onto my feet. I don't even fight him. Numbness has taken over my anger for the moment, and I let him guide me back to the house of omission.

We stop outside the front door, and I turn to him. "Why did you do it?" I ask. "How could you?" My voice cracks. A tear slides down my cheek, and I ask again. "Why?"

"I told you before, Luke, everything that I did was to protect you."

"Protect me?" I ask incredulously, wiping the second tear away. "I forgave you for talking me into something that I didn't want to do. I even forgave you for marrying *her*. But this? I don't know what to do with this. You stole my son. There's nothing right about that."

Jeremy watches me as I begin to pace back and forth across the porch.

"Did mom and dad know?" I ask.

"I told them when Jasper turned two, but you can't blame them, Luke. Mom has been trying to get us in the same room since she found out, but you…"

I swing around, stopping in front of Jeremy, and bunching his shirt in my fist. My other fist moves toward his face so fast that I barely recognize the movement. Jeremy dodges my hand before it makes contact with his face, and I lose my grip on his shirt. He stumbles back, his words lost and eyes widening.

"Don't you fucking dare try and place the blame on me. This is not on me." I hold my head between my palms, staring off in the distance. Then I drop my arms and walk over to the wooden beams, gripping the ledge beneath my hands, trying to hold onto what little control I still have.

I need to leave before I do something I'd regret.

"We need to talk about this, Luke," Jeremy says, his voice shaky.

I jerk my head in his direction. "What do you expect me to say, huh? That it's okay—you can keep pretending that my son is yours?" Jeremy gives me a solemn look. "Well, I don't know if I can." I close my eyes, then glance at the front door, shaking my head. "I can't go back in there. Not tonight. I need time to think. You owe me that much," I tell Jeremy, and he nods.

The urge to punch him is still too great. So, I step off the porch and head for my truck without another word. I can't add jail to my list of problems.

Chapter Nineteen

Rose

Luke only moved in with me a few days ago, and my home already feels lonely when he's gone. He's the best kind of roommate. He keeps my bed warm at night, my mind stimulated, my stomach full, and he's not bad to look at either. I wish I could keep him forever.

I've been home from work for a couple of hours now, and Luke's not home yet. I'm starting to get worried because I know he was meeting his brother tonight. From what he's told me about Jeremy, I don't think I'll be jumping at the chance to trust him any time soon. I got a weird vibe when I saw him. I guess I'd say that about all lawyers, though. All of the ones I know are creepy and unpredictable humans who are too good at their jobs and even better at keeping secrets.

I grab the remote, clicking through the channels on the muted television, attempting to distract myself for the umpteenth time tonight. Every channel is a reminder of all the bad things that Luke could be involved in right now, and I almost turn it off entirely before the hum of an engine reaches my ears.

I turn my head toward the light that now shines outside the living room window, my heartbeat picking up as relief washes over me. Five minutes pass before I hear the keys jingling at the door, and Luke enters. I widened my eyes at his appearance. His jeans and shirt are soaked, and his hair slicked back on his head as if he just stepped out of the shower. I've never seen him look so lost and broken in all of the time that I've known him. I guess I was right not to trust his brother.

"Luke," I call out his name, but it doesn't seem to register with him. It's like he doesn't even notice me. He keeps walking and goes into the guest bedroom, closing the door behind him. I want to follow him, but instead, I stay seated on the couch. Whatever it is, he will tell me when he's ready—at least I hope so.

Moments later, I hear the shower turn on. I grab a pillow and pull it to my chest for comfort. Minutes pass, and I keep glancing down the hallway and listening for the water to cease. I want to go to him, but I don't want to seem like an overbearing... I don't even know what to call myself since he's immune to titles. Whatever I am to him, I don't want to add overbearing to it.

The water finally turns off, and I release my grip on the pillow, putting it back in place next to me. My phone that I'd been checking for the last few hours dings, and I ignore it. The only thing that matters at the moment is whether Luke is okay.

I scoot to the edge of the chair and smile when I see him coming down the hallway with nothing but a towel tied around his waist and purpose in his steps. Luke doesn't return my smile as he approaches, and in turn, my smile disappears. I stand when he reaches me, and Luke immediately pulls me into his arms, hugging me close to his chest. His heartbeat pounds against my ear as he holds me, his chest tense at the side of my face.

Five Seconds. Ten. Fifteen. I lose track of how long we stand there wrapped in each other. I'm just glad that he came home to me.

Luke slowly releases me then cups my face in his hands. My heart cracks when I look into his red-stained eyes. He looks like he's been crying. In my experience, men cry because dying is the only other option, but it's not an option for them.

"Truth for a truth," he says in a strained voice.

I nod, leaning into his touch, feeling his pain, and hating the unknown.

"You are the only one that I trust completely with my heart," Luke says.

His words coat my skin with a warmth that I've never felt before, giving me a strength that I didn't know I had, and all I want to do is protect him from everything that dared to cause him harm.

A cloud of pain covers my eyes, but I blink it away. What the hell did his brother do to him? He has the look of someone who's been hurt again, and I wonder how much more he can take before he completely falls apart.

I place my palm on his bare chest, feeling his heartbeats reach out to me, and promise, "It will always be safe with me."

Luke tilts his head down to kiss me, his lips trembling but warm against mine. I'm so much more afraid of this feeling now. I'm worried that this thing that's tearing him apart is bringing us closer together. I'm so scared that my heart has reached the point of no return. It beats to his rhythm now. It sings and cries and laughs in tune with his, and it breaks because his heart is breaking. It hurts so bad and so good at the same time, but I refuse to run away.

I throw my arms around his neck and kiss him back. His hands caress my back, sending chills across my skin, then slide down to cup my ass. I gasp when he squeezes, lifting me in one swift move. I cross my ankles behind his back as he walks us over to the wall, pressing my back against it. I can feel his need rising beneath the towel until it presses hard against my center.

Luke pulls away from my lips, confessing, "I need you, Petals. I want you," he says, one hand landing on the wall beside my head. "Can I have you?" he asks, trailing kisses down my neck, and I breathe out, "Yes."

Luke steps back an inch, allowing my feet to touch the floor. He removes my shorts and panties, then pulls my shirt over my head. My breathing is sparse as his eyes roam over my body.

"Beautiful," he says, sliding the back of his fingers over my cheeks, then down my arms. "I don't deserve you," he says. "You deserve better."

I shake my head no and touch my finger to his lips, because how can he possibly think that? "I deserve *you*," I tell him. "I want *you*." I release the towel from his waist and run a finger up his shaft. "Let me be there for you. Let me be the one to give you what you need." At this moment, I do not doubt that what he needs is me because he told me so.

Luke rolls a condom on and gazes at me with a war in his eyes before lifting me back against the wall. My arms go around his neck again, then he reaches between us and slowly slips himself inside of me, releasing a grunt as he does. He braces his hand on the wall, the other hand gripping my thigh as he pauses inside me. The tip of his nose brushes the base of my neck before his eyes return to mine. I let out a soft moan when he pulled my nipple between his teeth teasingly. He begins to move in and out of me, his movements controlled like he's holding back. I want him to let go.

"I'm yours, Luke. Let go," I whisper into his ear.

My words seem to release him from his torture, and he slams into me, deliciously so. "Yes," I say, urging him on. He gives me his pain under the guise of pleasure, drowning me in it until my breath catches and his body stills. He grunts into me one last time, his head falling to my shoulder. A few seconds pass before he slides out of me completely. My knees buckle when my feet touch the floor, so I clutch Luke's shoulders to keep from falling. Then he lifts me into his arms, kisses the side of my head, and takes me to bed.

I try to keep my eyes open, but it's no use. Exhaustion overtakes me and my words. The last thought that I have is tomorrow. We'll talk tomorrow.

Chapter Twenty

Luke

I broke my promise.

Rose was the only thought on my mind last night during the moment when it mattered. But before and after, all I could think about was that innocent little boy and how Jeremy lied to keep him from me. My past is nowhere near sorted, and I feel like shit for using Rose to drown out some of the noise.

I don't know what to do.

I have a son, but he doesn't even know that I exist. The decision to fight for him might have been easier if he were still a baby, but he's five. Jeremy is the only father he's ever known. It would break his little heart to be torn away from him. I know because it's breaking my heart to even think about ignoring what I know.

I'm not sure if I should tell Rose or just let her go. This might all be too much for her. She wasn't expecting a kid that's not hers. I'm not even sure if she wants kids. The thought of having a kid hadn't even crossed my mind until this happened.

I want to tell her, but I'm even more afraid of losing her now than before. Dalton sent a group text last night confirming our plans to Justin. Our ride leaves in a few hours, and that's not the sort of news you spring on someone, then leave them to sort it out on their own. I haven't even told her about the show tomorrow yet. This whole being accountable for my whereabouts will take some getting used to if I continue with Rose.

I woke up before the sun this morning again. Instead of staring at Rose for hours as I'd done the last time, I slipped on a pair of shorts, made coffee, and poured myself a cup. Now I'm sitting outside on the back steps away from prying eyes with a slight breeze brushing my bare chest. The vinyl fence is high enough that no one would know I'm here unless I made a lot of noise and the sky is just beginning to shed a little light.

I sip down the final bit of my coffee and sit the cup on the step next to me.

"Good morning."

I turn when I hear Rose's voice behind me. She's standing inside the door frame with a robe wrapped around her.

"Good morning." I smile, then pat the space next to me. She has to be at work in a little while, but I need her next to me now that she's awake.

Rose comes closer, walking down two steps, and I reach my hand up to assist her.

"Another night without sleep?" she asks.

I nod, kissing the side of her head. "Didn't want to wake you."

Rose watches me expectantly, her smile a little happy and a little sad. I can tell that she wants to know what happened last night—why I looked like I had been through a storm, but I just can't. Not yet.

"The band's leaving in a couple of hours," I tell her.

She tilts her head in confusion. "Today? I thought you guys were going to wait until the new year," she says.

"We were, but we talked about it. We're all a little restless," I say, bracing my elbows on my knees. "It's only until Sunday. It'll be good to get away from this place for a few days."

I watch her closely, gauging her reaction. She twists her lips to the side in thought, her eyes falling deeper into sadness. "Okay," she says, sounding unsure. "Yeah, it'll be good for you to get away."

The look on her face mirrors my dilemma. I want to go on this trip, but I don't want to leave her behind. I need her with me.

I take her hand in mine. "Why don't you come with me?" I suggest.

Rose's eyes widened in surprise. "Come with you?" she asks, pausing as if she's considering it.

"Yeah," I answer, putting an arm around her and nibbling on her ear. "You could be my groupie. We could share a room and let one thing lead to another."

Rose giggles, and her shoulder nudges my chin near her ear. "I can't. I have work, and it's such short notice. I just started a new job," she rambles.

I move away from her ear and give her hand a light squeeze. "It was just a suggestion," I say disappointingly. I knew she wouldn't go for it, but I had to try. Her being with me would've made my decision about what to do a lot easier, but I understand. Rose had a life before me—one that I'd never ask her to give up. I wouldn't want to ruin a good thing for her.

"I wish I could come to see you in action on the big stage," she says with a small smile.

"Maybe another time then," I say, placing a chaste kiss on her lips.

Rose touches my cheek with her palm. "I hate leaving you like this, but I don't want to be late. Will you let me know that you've arrived safely?" she asks.

"I will. Now go before I change my mind."

Rose stands, and our hands drift apart as she walks back into the house.

I fell asleep in the back of the bus on the way to the hotel. I don't open my eyes until Frank pulls us into a dark parking garage that's supposed to be private. I don't move until Dean knocks my foot off the tiny bed, telling me it's time.

Justin rented us a bus for the trip and secured the hotel's top floor, saying he'll meet us here. The show is scheduled for tomorrow, and it's supposed to be a big crowd. So, we brought my new guy, Russell, along for the ride. It'll be his first time guarding against a huge crowd, but I know he'll do great.

The valet service takes care of our bags, removing them from the bus and taking them to our rooms. They must be under strict instructions because they barely give us eye contact.

I'm still bummed about Rose not being able to come, but it feels good to be miles away from my family and the problems that await me back in Cane.

"Everything okay, Luke?" Owen asks once we're in the elevator.

I can't lie to him. He knows me well enough to know that something is wrong, but I'm not ready to talk about it yet. I'm still trying to process it myself. That, and we're not alone in the elevator. Dalton is next to him, which I wouldn't mind sharing with him, but our security is with us as well. They're like family to us, but we've never disclosed our secrets to them.

"I'd rather not talk about it right now," I respond.

The elevator door dings on the top floor and we exit freely, going to our rooms.

Owen stops outside his door and turns to me. "I'm here when you're ready," he says, and I nod, stepping inside my room and closing the door.

I pull out my phone and send Rose a message letting her know that we've arrived. Then, I lie on the bed for hours with my sticks in my hands, staring up at the ceiling with my earbuds in, letting music control my thoughts.

I startle when I feel something push at my foot. Justin is standing over me with an irritated look on his face.

Justin always has a key to each of our rooms in case of an emergency. So, I don't bother asking how he got in.

"Why are you in here?" I ask him.

"We've been trying to call you for the past thirty minutes. Dinner's here, and we need to prep for tomorrow. Let's go," he demands and turns for the door.

I smirk after him, impressed with myself for riling him up. I get up and follow him to a room down the hall that he had set up as a meeting space where we could all be in one place. For the next two hours, we eat and go over the show for tomorrow. Then we return to our rooms.

I check my phone backstage before slipping it into my pocket. I had expected Rose to return my text last night, but there's still silence on her end. I'm starting to believe she's having second thoughts. I probably would be if I were in her shoes dealing with a guy like me.

"Time to get your head in the game," Dalton says, forcibly palming my shoulder.

He stops beside me, and Owen stops at my other side. The noise from the crowd reaches us from behind the tall silver curtains.

"I'm here," I say as I take it all in—the lights, the screams, the smell of faux smoke on stage. I jump up and down two times, shaking my wrists and cracking my neck as if I'm preparing for a fight. "Let's go."

We make our way on stage and take our positions. I kiss my index finger, holding it up to the sky, saying a silent prayer. Then the curtain begins to rise.

As soon as the tip of my sticks caresses the face of my drums, the screams seem to get louder, and I'm pulled back in as if we'd never left. My hands move of their own accord, wrists flicking, every note struck with precision. I move my foot to the rhythm, pounding the pedal—the mallet pelting against the bass below. The beat carries me, moving my body along with it, and sweat begins to trickle down the side of my face. Song after song, I feel more at home, but I can't quite reach the full feeling. Something's missing. Someone is missing, but at the same time, I realize that the missing may be the part that I have to let go of for good.

The music stops, and the curtain lowers. We go backstage to the dressing room and sign autographs as usual. Then we hop into a rental and attend an afterparty at one of the local clubs.

It's strange being in VIP, just the guys and me sitting around sipping on our drinks. It wasn't that long ago that I'd preferred to have a female on my lap at these outings.

The crowd isn't as appealing as it once was because there's only one woman that I want to spend my time with, and she's not here. Maybe this is a sign that our lives are too different for this ever to work.

I glance over at Dalton, who seems to have settled into his life quite nicely, but we've always been different people. I always knew he'd be the first to have a family of his own. My eyes move to Owen, who's watching the crowd. If the right person came along, he could settle down tonight without a second thought. I want to be that guy. I was trying to be that guy for Rose, but I feel like I'd be hindering her. I notice the worried looks she gives me, and that's no way to start a relationship.

Owen leans his head over to me, shouting above the music. "Not the same, huh?" he asks.

"Pssh. I feel like I've aged ten years in the past month," I respond, taking a sip from my glass and resting it back on my knee. "Can't believe I ever enjoyed this. I mean, we should be enjoying this, right? We're twenty-four-year-old musicians in a room full of women, and we can have any one of them if we wanted to, but look at us."

Owen stares at me for a moment, then he says, "It's called growing up, living life and not letting life live you."

"But why now?" I ask. *Why would someone be thrown into my path only to be ripped away?* "And why, Rose?" I ask quietly. *What's the point in knowing her if I'd be faced with such an impossible choice?* It's like the universe is playing a sick joke on me. It seems the higher she climbs, the lower I fall. We're moving in different directions.

Owen leans in the opposite direction toward Dalton, saying something that I can't hear, and Dalton nods. Dalton looks over his head, waving Dean down with two fingers while Owen says, "We've made an appearance. Let's get out of here."

I have no cause to object. This is the last place that I want to be right now. It's definitely time to talk about renegotiating our contract. I finish the last of my drink, then set the glass down and stand. I ignore the whispers and eyes that follow us as we leave because none of it matters.

I recheck my phone on the way to the hotel, and still nothing from Rose. Dalton beat me to the back far rear seat, so I'm sitting next to Owen. He's giving me that look again, like he knows something no one else knows. The last time he looked at me that way, Rose walked into a reception with another guy.

"Alright, what did you do?" I ask him.

He smirks with a shrug but doesn't answer. I don't even have the energy to try and argue it out of him. So, I let it go, lay my head on the back of the seat, and close my eyes.

A few minutes later, we're back in the garage of the hotel. I now know the true meaning of *going through the motions*. My mind is a mix of hurt and fury. Being on the elevator barely registers with me until it dings for us to exit on our floor. I stand up straight from leaning against the railing inside the elevator, keeping my eyes to the floor. The small piece of home that I'd found on stage is barely there anymore, and every thought that I'd tried to push away is regaining its power inside my head and heart. My feet move down the dimly lit corridor, stopping when I reach my room.

I glance over at Owen. He nods, giving me that same look he had in the truck, and steps inside his room. I stick my keycard into the slot until I hear the lock click. Then, I step inside, and the door closes behind me automatically.

I freeze at the same moment the door clicks, and she rises from the bed.

Rose.

"I hope you don't mind," she says. "I wanted to surprise you." Her palms turn up beside her head, her shoulders rising with them.

"How did you?" I pause, swallowing hard. I can't believe she came.

"I had a lot of help from Owen and Justin. They whisked me here after work. It's not as easy as I thought, trying to talk my way into a star's room. So much red tape," she jokes, taking a step toward me and stopping as she examines the look of shock and confusion on my face.

I walk further inside, moving past her to face the sliding glass door with Rose behind me. I close my eyes for a few seconds then open them. Then I hear her say, "I shouldn't have come. I'm sorry."

I can feel her right behind me now, and I turn, pulling her into my arms. "Don't be sorry. I'm glad you came, Petals. I just…" I needed her, and she came. That has to be a sign, right? That somehow, she knew I needed her with me?

I close my eyes over her shoulder, enjoying the feel of her in my arms again. I am glad that she came, however unexpected it is. I breathe her in, the feeling of home enveloping me once more. I pull my head up to look at her, really look at her. Then, I rub my thumb over her cheek as my fingers rest at the back of her neck.

"My God, you're beautiful and sexy, and you're here," I say.

"You guys were great tonight," Rose says.

"You saw the show?" I ask, my brows scrunching together.

"I did, and I came back here afterward," she shrugs. "Didn't want to interrupt anything you had going," she says, looking away.

I guide her face back to me and look deep into her eyes. "There is nowhere else or anyone else I'd rather be with. Trust that."

I run my thumb over her bottom lip, then tilt my head to kiss her. Rose opens her mouth to me, and my tongue snakes inside, finding hers. My hand tightens on her waist, my fingers on her neck drawing her closer. Her tongue mingles with mine, the taste of mint teasing my senses. Rose moans as she clutches my shirt in her hands between us. The way she responds to my touch makes me want all of her, but I won't have her again. Not until she knows the whole truth. Not until I decide what I want to do. I slow the kiss, sucking her bottom lip into my mouth as I reluctantly pull away.

"Now that," Rose pauses, biting at her lip, "was a proper greeting," she finishes.

My lips turn up, and a chuckle escapes me. "You can thank the woman in the mirror next time you see her. She makes me feel things I've never felt before and do things I've never done."

How could I ever give you up? I ask Rose silently.

I decide at that exact moment that I don't want to. I'm here for her until she tells me to stop. If things don't work out between us, it will be because she made it so. Rose has made me strong, but she is also my weakness, and I can't let her go on my own.

Chapter Twenty-One

Luke

I thought it would be easier to break the news to Rose once we were back home, but it's not. It's even harder. I could've told her when she showed up at the hotel last night, but the car ride home this morning would've been awkward.

I spent most of the day skirting around the issue as we hung out around the house. It's such a beautiful day that we decide to spend the evening outside. I've been sitting on a blanket I'd spread out beside one of the tall trees in the back yard with my back perched against it. My head is tilted toward the sky, and my eyes are closed behind dark-tinted shades.

"I've been thinking," Rose says, shimmying her shoulders from side to side as she lay across my lap. "I haven't seen my parents in a while. Time just sort of got away from me; you know?"

I look down at her, but I can barely see her eyes behind the dark shades she's wearing.

"So, I thought I'd go see them tomorrow," she continues. "And maybe you could come with me." I feel her body tense on my legs. Then she adds, "That's if you want to. If you're not busy."

I stay quiet, thankful for the cover of darkness over my eyes. Grateful that she can't see what I'm feeling. I would love nothing more than to meet her parents, but she may change her mind about me going once she finds out the truth. I tip my head back on the tree once more, my heart hurting for more reasons than one. I was afraid of the way I was falling for her, but now I'm even more fearful of losing her.

"Rose," I say, running my fingers through her hair. "I need to tell you something," I pause, getting choked up by my thoughts. "And when I'm done, I need you to do something for me."

"Anything," Rose says without hesitation. Though, I'm not sure she would have said it if she knew what I needed.

She tries to sit up, but I say, "Please stay," guiding her back down. I don't want to see the look in her eyes when I tell her.

"When I'm done, don't think about me. I need you to be selfish—think about you and what it all means."

She ignores my plea for her to stay where she is and sits up. She faces me and removes her shades, and I have to look away. Her hand lands on my thigh, and she makes no promises when she says, "Tell me," just as she'd done the last time.

There's a fierceness, a determination in her voice that tells me she won't do what I asked. Rose is the most selfless person that I know, but just this once, I wish that she would put her first.

I'd been trying to figure out a way to tell her, but the timing is never right, and there is no easy way. I don't start by telling her everything that I feel for her because that would only make her want to stay. I don't wrap the news in a box and decorate it with a bow because it's not pretty. I spit it out like the vile, wicked thing that it is.

"I have a son, Rose, and my brother kept him from me."

Rose's intake of breath hits my ears, and I suck in a breath of my own. Saying it out loud again hurts worse than thinking it—it makes it too real.

Rose jerks her hand away from me, and even then, I still can't bring myself to look at her—to see the rejection on her face.

"He's five years old, the little boy that you saw the other night," I continue speaking. "Five. And I've never met him," I pause, taking a deep breath. I can feel my eyes tearing up, my heartbeats so loud that I can hear the pounding in my ears. I remove the shades from my eyes and lay them next to me, pinching the bridge of my nose to try and ward off the pain to no avail.

I try not to be selfish, to hold it inside, but my voice cracks out, "It hurts. It fucking hurts so bad." I close my eyes, then the tears begin to fall, and I finally let myself grieve.

I still can't bring myself to look at Rose, but I feel that she's still near me. I want to touch her—for her to give me the strength that I need, but I can't make this decision for her.

I feel Rose's hand on my cheek, her thumb wiping at my tears. Then she pulls me to her, and I drop my head weakly into the crook of her neck. There's no shame in my tears that wet her skin—only affliction, and Rose holds me, not seeming to mind either way.

Rose reiterates her claim, whispering in my ear, "You don't have to do this alone. I'm here. I'm here, Luke."

At that moment, I knew that our truths were more than just simple truths. They are promises that we made to one another—promises that Rose intends to keep, even when faced with my hardest truth yet. I also know that I can't let her do it. I won't let her put me before herself, regardless of how much I want her to.

I feel like a young boy again when I pull away from her, wiping at my eyes with the back of my hands.

"Rose," I say, lifting my hand to her arm. "Walk away from me."

She blanches, her eyes taking on a hurtful hue. "But..." She starts then stops talking, glancing away from me for a moment.

"My life is so fucked up right now, Rose. I can't be who you need me to be," I lie. "I want you to go." My heart tightens in my chest. "See your parents," I add. "I have to do this on my own."

Her eyes search mine pleadingly, and I know that my excuse is not enough. She'll never leave if I don't push harder. Rose is a fighter, and she'll go to war to keep me unless I break her heart.

"Truth for a truth?" I ask her.

"Yes, please," she implores.

I swallow deeply. My thoughts are like acid on my tongue, burning before they reach the sound.

"Being with you is only making this harder," I say.

It's the truth. With Rose in the picture, everything is more complicated. I have to put in more time, more thought, more of everything because my decisions aren't just made for me. The only way she can help me with this decision is to make one of her own.

If she decides that with me is where she wants to be after she gives it some thought, she will make me the happiest broken man alive. And if she decides otherwise, I'll accept it—still broken, but at least I'd know she's happy.

I kiss her forehead, my lips lingering there for a bit. Then I pull back to look into her eyes and let go of her arm.

My mind screams for Rose to tell me I'm wrong—to say to me she's not leaving me, but I can see the fight slowly leaving her eyes. My words have imprinted on her heart. She's hurt. The look on her face is even worse than it was when she spoke of the other guy that hurt her.

Rose stares back at me, then places her hand on my cheek as she begins to speak.

"All I'll ever want is for you to be happy," she speaks her truth, her voice sad and defeated. "If you're not happy, say the words, and I'll go. I'll do what you ask."

"I'm not happy," I force out, nearly choking on the words. What I don't mention is that it's not because of her. She's the only one who makes me happy. I always knew I had a heart, but I didn't appreciate the way it beats until Rose came along.

"Okay," Rose says, her hand falling away from my face. She stands up and smooths her hands over the back of her pants. She starts to walk away, then stops, looking back at me. "Will you do something for me while I'm gone?" she asks.

"Anything," I say truthfully.

"Figure out what it is you want, Luke, or you'll be stuck in the past forever, and there will be no one to blame but yourself. Decide for you," she says, throwing my words back at me. Then she disappears inside the house.

I stay outside under the tree, peering up at the sky until the sun begins to fade. The feeling of loss is too great to measure and too hard to own up to. I feel like shit for treating Rose that way, but I care about her too much to let her make a rash decision for someone like me. She deserves so much more than what I can give her.

I stand up and run my hands through my hair.

"What the fuck am I doing?" I ask, but no one is there to answer.

I grab the blanket from the ground and walk toward the house. When I get inside, the door to Rose's bedroom is closed. So, I join my clothes in the guest bedroom, not wanting to bother her. To be honest, I'm not sure if we're still together or not. I never said that I didn't want her, only that I wasn't happy, and she should walk away from me.

I throw the blanket on the floor, then lie on the bed with my arm folded over my eyes. I keep asking myself the same question repeatedly because I don't understand what I did to deserve this. How did my life get so fucked up?

I toss and turn most of the night, only getting about two hours of sleep in between wakes. I finally give in and get up just before seven. The house is so quiet, and I wonder if Rose got any sleep last night or if she was just as tormented as me.

I stop outside her room door with my knuckle paused against it, needing to see her before she leaves, even though it was my suggestion that she go away without me. I draw in a deep breath and knock, but there's no answer. I put my ear to the door and knocked again and still nothing, so I opened the door. The bed is fully made, and the silence hits me harder than it ever has before.

She's gone.

She's gone, and my future with her hangs in the balance.

I didn't think that my heart could break anymore, but it is. It hurt, telling Rose to go, but I made the right decision. I have to do this on my own. I still have no clue what I want to do about the kid, but maybe seeing him will give me some sort of clue and help me make the right decision.

I perch my back against the door jamb and pull out my phone, firing off a text to Jeremy.

Me: Meet me at Mom's in an hour. Bring the kid. I pause, adding, *And Marcia.* Then hit send.

A few seconds pass before Jeremy reads my message, and the dots begin to wave. Then one word follows.

Jeremy: Okay.

I juggle the phone in my hand for a moment, my nerves getting the best of me, then I stand and walk into the kitchen. I grab the refrigerator's handle and notice a note on the board from Rose before opening it. All it says is, *"I'll be back tonight."*

Even without knowing where we stand, her note somehow makes me smile. The fact that she was thinking of me on her way out the door gives me hope at a time when I should have none.

Chapter Twenty-Two

Rose

I barely slept last night with Luke's new reality swirling through my mind. I wanted to go to him, to tell him again that I'm here. His eyes were practically begging me to say the words when I last saw him, but I couldn't because he's right. As much as I want to help him through this, it's a life-changing decision.

If Luke decides to fight for his child, I would inevitably be taking on the responsibility too. My career is just starting to flourish. Where would I find the time to entertain a child? What kind of strain would something like that put on our relationship? I imagine it will be taxing with Luke being on the road, but this?

And even if he doesn't, the guilt of knowing will always be there in the back of his mind, and I'd be tasked with picking up the pieces. There is no right answer for this.

I guess the big question is, am I ready for that? I honestly have no clue, but for Luke, I'm willing to try.

I shrunk away from Luke when he first told me, and I regret my reaction—not that it wasn't a normal action because the news was shocking. I regret it because for one moment, I let my confidence slip. I made him feel as if he had done something wrong. I made him feel like my feelings at that moment were more important than his truth, and for that, I am sorry.

I knew that seeing him this morning would only make me want to stay. So, I wrote him a note and left without saying goodbye.

My mom and dad moved an hour away, further into the wilderness once I'd gotten settled during my college years. The drive didn't seem that long on the way here, and I can't believe it's taken me months to visit again.

The garage door is up when I pull into the driveway. Mom turns in my direction away from the shelve she'd been meddling with. Her smile is just as bright as I remembered it. I cut the car off and step out of the car, then move toward her open arms.

"What a surprise," she says, wrapping her arms completely around me. "I was wondering why your call hadn't come yet."

"It's good to see you, mom," I say as she pulls away to look at me.

Her eyes run over me approvingly until they land on my face. She stares into my eyes, examining me. Her hand comes up to my cheek, and it's as if she knows before I even say anything. Her smile cuts in half, and she grabs my hand.

"Come inside. I'll make us some tea," Mom says, guiding me into the house.

Mom washes her hands and starts a pot of tea, then grabs two mugs along with some cream and sugar. I sit at the kitchen table, watching her with a sad smile on my face. I didn't know how much I'd missed her until now. It's crazy how I didn't realize it until something came along to remind me.

She sets the mug in front of me, pouring the steamy liquid inside. Then she pours one for herself and sits across from me.

"Thank you," I tell her, and she nods, taking a sip from her mug.

Mom doesn't pry or try to pull the information from me. She just sits there and waits for my move. She knows that being here with her is solace enough—it's giving me what I need without the need for words to be spoken—at least until I'm ready.

"Is dad around?" I ask.

"No. He had to run out for a bit. He should be back in a little while. I wish I'd know you were coming. I would've had him pick something up to cook."

"You don't have to go to all that trouble for me. It's not why I came," I respond, looking down at the mug between my hands and back up. "I just wanted to see you, a touch of home."

"Well, I'm glad you came," she says, still studying me.

"Can I ask you a question, Mom?"

"Sure."

"How did you know that dad was the one you wanted to spend your forever with?"

Mom smiles and looks off into the distance as if she remembers something. Then her eyes fall on me again.

"I didn't," she says simply. "Your father was a pain in my side. I think he decided for me, and I just sort of went along with it. He would tease me, then ignore me. His actions were confusing to the point where I thought I hated him, but then something happened," she pauses, a small giggle bubbling out of her.

"What happened?"

"I started to show interest in this other guy, and your father started paying attention. He didn't like it one bit, and he told me as much. Of course, I was stubborn, but your father was persistent. He told the other guy to get lost and told me that I was his girl."

"And the rest is history?" I ask.

"No, not exactly. I didn't want the other guy anymore, considering how easy he'd given up. I also didn't like your father telling me what to do. The idea of being his girl was kind of exciting, but someone had to teach him a lesson. So, I played hard to get, and in time he learned how I wanted to be treated. And that's how our history began. It hasn't always been smooth sailing, but we've had a good life."

"Wow," I say. "But you guys always made it look so easy."

"It was good, not easy," mom corrects. "Anything worth having and keeping takes effort. If it comes too easy, it'll go just as quickly."

I finally take a sip from my mug, thinking about Luke and the hardness of his situation—realizing that I could be the one to help him through it. I've always known that I could, but he asked me for this one thing—to think of myself first, and I've done that. I want to be with him regardless of what decision he makes. I'd choose hard with him over easy with someone else any day. But the real question is, Will he choose me?

I set my mug down on the table, cracking a smile. "Thanks, mom, for always knowing just the right thing to say."

Mom tilts her head a little. "I'm not sure where all of this is coming from, but I do know my daughter, and I know you'll make the best decision for you."

"I will," I say, confirming her assumption.

"Now," she says, reaching her hand across the table for mine. "Tell me about this Luke of yours."

Mom always knew I had a crush on Luke, even when I was in high school. So, when I messaged her earlier this week that we were dating, she's been dying to know more ever since. I didn't give anything away, feeling that news like that was better discussed in person. It's one of the reasons why I wanted to come and why I wanted to bring Luke with me—so she could see how happy I am. So she could meet the guy who stole my heart a long time ago.

I spend the next few minutes telling mom about all the parts of Luke that aren't messy. How he's learning how to treat me. How he put me before himself. How he claims to be falling in love with me. My heart swells with every word because it remembers. A heart never forgets the way someone makes it feel.

Then I helped mom finish organizing her shelves in the garage, as I'd interrupted her when I arrived. When dad comes home, I give him a huge hug and spend some time with him, pulling weeds from beside the house. He's happy for the company more than anything, and it reminds me of when I was younger—when I didn't want to do yard work, but he'd make me do it anyway. I always complained that it was a boy's chore, but dad always insisted that it wasn't. I'm realizing now that maybe he just wanted to spend time with me, and it's not as bad a chore as I thought. It's not a chore at all. It's calming.

Before I leave, I promise them that I wouldn't stay away so long before visiting again. Then I pull away with one track on my mind—finding out what Luke really wants.

Chapter Twenty-Three

Luke

The sky is different today. The sun is hiding behind white clouds, but there is no threat of a storm. Even the storm inside me has calmed as I walk up to the front door of my parent's home. The weight still rests heavily on me, but the urge to kill has subsided. I'm here to decide the future of an innocent little boy.

I step inside, and the chill in the air immediately hits me. This house has never felt so cold before. It seems to be an increasing staple with each visit.

Jeremy and Marcia straighten as I enter the living room. I look around for Jasper, but he's not there. I take a deep breath.

"Where's the kid?" I ask because he's the reason I'm here. I want to meet him. Whether I decide that he's my son or Jeremy's, he'll always be in my life. That's the most challenging part about all of this. It will hurt me either way.

"With mom and dad," Jeremy says.

"We thought it would be best if we talked first," Marcia says, and my eyes cut to her. She clears her throat, looking away from me. So, I look at Jeremy.

My hands balled into fists at my side. Then I sit down across from them, willing to hear them out.

"I know why you did it, Jeremy, which is still fucked up, by the way. But you, Marcia, what did I do to you to deserve any of this?" I ask, gesturing to the two of them. "Why go after my brother? Why didn't you just take the money and disappear?"

"I didn't mean for this to happen, Luke," Marcia says. "All I wanted was what I asked for, but then I found out I was pregnant. I knew that you'd do the right thing—that you'd take care of it, even if it meant making it go away," she says, hanging her head in shame. Her eyes climb back up slowly, then she continues. "I had no way of contacting you aside from Jeremy, so I called him. I told him I needed to speak with you, that I needed more money, but he refused. He said he realized that the only way to protect you from me was to keep me close. So, he suggested that we get married. That would take blackmail off the table, I would be taken care of, and you would never have to know why we did it. I wasn't thinking rationally, so I agreed. It wasn't until after we were married that I told him about Jasper. I wanted to tell you, but I felt so guilty for everything else I had done by that time. I didn't want to ruin your career as I'd threatened to do with Jeremy. So, we decided to raise him as our own."

"So, you decided to raise my child with my brother—a child that you weren't even sure you wanted? You made the decision for me?" I grip the arm of the chair, my emotions rising. I continue but try to keep my voice leveled because of the kid lurking around. "Did either of you stop to think about what it would do to Jasper when he finds out? If he were to be ripped away from you because of it?"

Marcia sucks in a breath, her body lurching forward, but Jeremy stops her. It's the only action I've understood from her since I met her. At least I know she feels something for someone other than herself.

"No. You can't," Marcia pleads.

I smirk. "You're wrong, Marcia. I can, and you two idiots have put me in an incontestable position to win if I tried." Marcia's eyes go wide, her head turning to Jeremy, and my eyes slide over to him. "Right, brother?" If anyone knows the workings of the law in this room, it's him.

"Luke, think about this. You don't want to put Jasper in the middle of this. He will hate you for the rest of his life," Jeremy tries to reason with me.

"I didn't put him in the middle of anything. You did. The way I see it, he'll hate me either way," I shrug, finally feeling an ounce of power course through me. "I want to meet my son," I say with finality. We've said everything that needs to be said between us for now. "I need to meet him before I move forward."

Jeremy hesitates for a moment, then he and Marcia stand. At least they're united, I think to myself.

"They're out back," he says as he begins to walk out of the living room.

I follow behind them, keeping a small distance between us. The closer I get to the back door, the more my nerves creep forward.

Jasper runs up to Jeremy when we step outside, yelling, "Daddy!"

The excitement and love in his voice are undeniable. I want to be mad, but it's not the kid's fault because he doesn't know.

"Jasper, I'd like you to meet someone," Jeremy says to him. He grabs his hand and guides him over to me. There's an unreadable question on Jeremy's face as they stop in front of me. I realize he doesn't know how to introduce me. What title to give me.

I kneel to Jasper's level, and he just stares at me. I didn't pay much attention to him the last time that I saw him because I was too upset about seeing Marcia again, but being this close to him now, he looks so much like me. He also bears a resemblance to Jeremy. If they hadn't told me he was mine, I wouldn't have questioned it.

"Daddy, who's that man?" Jasper asks, poking a knife at my heart.

I would never have thought that a child of mine would refer to me as that man. Jeremy really fucked things up. I can't imagine that there's anything else he can do to make me feel more broken than I already am.

"Hey, Jasper. I'm his brother." I cut in before Jeremy can answer, pointing my thumb in his direction.

"Oh," he says, wrinkling his little nose. He squints his eyes, getting a better look at me. "I remember you from the firework party."

I chuckle a little at how keen he is. So much like me at that age. I hardly noticed him, but he was obviously watching all of us. I'm glad I walked away that night.

"You're a smart kid Jasper. You must be..." I pause, bringing my finger to my chin in faux thought. "Three," I finish, and it surprises me how easy it is to talk to him, even though I've missed out on so much. I've heard that once you have a child, your parental instincts automatically kick in. I guess mine has been lying dormant all of these years until now.

"I'm not three. I'm five," Jasper says proudly, poking out his chest and tilting his chin up.

I chuckle again, and my heart skips a beat at how proud I am of this kid that I don't know—proud of who he already is.

"Well, Jasper, I have an idea," I say to him. "If you show me what you were doing over there, I bet I could help you get it done faster. What do you think?"

Jasper grips Jeremy's hand tighter, his head tilting up to look at him. Jeremy smiles down at him and says, "It's okay, bud. He's not a stranger."

But the fact that he has to say those words makes me feel like one. I feel like the biggest stranger here.

"Okay, you can help, but I'm in charge," Jasper says.

I stand up, looking around at my family, but I don't feel at home. I follow Jasper over to where he was playing earlier. Then I sit down next to Jasper and let him instruct me on how to build a truck with Lego blocks. It's hard to live in the moment when the entire time my mind is muddled with all of the things that I've missed—his cries, his first words, his first steps, his first day of school—all of the time I'll never get back.

When we're done, I know what I have to do. I have to let Jasper go. I can't be his father because he already has one, but I can be the best uncle he'll ever have until our truth turns him against me. For now, it will have to be enough. I won't turn Jasper's life inside out because, at this point, it would be selfish of me. He wouldn't understand it.

I follow Jeremy and Marcia back inside when I'm ready to leave. Every step I take away from Jasper feels like goodbye. I'll see him again, I'm sure, but I guess it is goodbye in a way because I'm burying any thoughts of being his father.

"What are you going to do?" Jeremy asks me once we're behind closed doors. I've never seen fear so prominent in his eyes. He's usually not afraid of anything, but I see it clearly—he's worried that I'll take his son away.

I turn my back for a few seconds, running my hands through my hair, hating the words before they form.

"Fuck," I whisper-shout.

My hands trail through my hair again, palms resting at the back of my neck. Then, I turn back around to face them, dropping my arms to my side in defeat.

"As much as it pains me to say this, I want Jasper to have the best life, and right now, that's with you. I'll be uncle Luke to him," I croak out, and the words seem dirty leaving my mouth. "I'll have to find a way to live with that," I manage to say without malice. "I don't find any pleasure in knowing that one day he'll hate you just as much as he'll hate me. All I ask is that you raise him right, and when that day comes, don't you dare give up on him. Tell him what you told me—that everything we did was to protect him. Tell him I've loved him since the day we met."

I pause, glancing at the back door. It's true. I love that little boy. I don't even know where the feeling came from, but it's alive inside of me.

"He may not understand it," I continue. "And he'll want to beat the shit out of you, but eventually, he'll come around."

I stare into Jeremy's eyes, making sure he understands my hidden message, and he nods. I don't understand today, but maybe one day I'll be able to. Maybe one day, I'll be able to be around him and think of him as my brother again. Just don't give up fighting for me.

I feel some of the weight lift when I step outside. We still have a long way to go, but we're one step closer to healing.

When I got into my truck, I sent Owen a message asking if I could crash at his place, and he responded, yes. Then I sent Rose a text informing her that I'm staying at Owen's and wouldn't be home tonight.

With Jeremy's issue as resolved as it can be, it's freed up time for me to think about Rose and what I want with her. The next time I see her, I want to be clear about what that is, and I want to make it clear to her too.

Owen opens the door for me when I arrive, then walks away, leaving me to close it behind me.

"Trouble in paradise already?" He jokes.

"I don't exactly know, but I'm hoping I can clear everything up," I tell him. "I need to fill you and Dalton in on something tomorrow, and I also need your help with another thing."

"Okay," Owen says, watching me suspiciously.

"Tomorrow," I promise. "Tonight, I just need to sleep. Feels like I haven't done that in weeks," I say.

Chapter Twenty-Four

Luke

Since I knew Rose would be at work, Owen and I stopped by her house for me to freshen up before going to Dalton's.

We get a few hours of practice in once we arrive. Then I fill them in on the latest with Jeremy and me. Surprised doesn't begin to describe their reactions when I told them. They were supportive of my decision, though, as I knew they would be.

"So, what's this other thing you wanted to discuss?" Dalton asks, wiping at his neck with a towel. He's standing in the open garage thruway with his back to Owen and me. Owen is leaning against the left wall, and I'm sitting on an overturned bucket.

"It's about Rose," I say.

Dalton glances over his shoulder, then does a complete turn toward me. "What about her?"

"I want to marry her," I say without hesitation. "Before you say anything, hear me out. With everything that happened the last few weeks, I feel like I'm on a legit losing streak. Rose is the only aspect of my life where I feel like I have some sort of control. Besides music and you guys, she's the only true thing I have going for me."

I see Owen's head snap in my direction out of the corner of my eye while Dalton watches me curiously.

"I know what you're both thinking. That it's too fast. That I'm not thinking clearly, but it's not, and I am. I love Rose, and I want to hold on to that feeling. I don't want to lose her too."

Dalton takes a step toward me and stops, hanging his towel over his shoulder but not letting go. "Are you sure about this?" he asks. "A lot has happened in the last few days with you. Enough to drive anyone insane. Marriage is a big step and shouldn't be taken lightly."

I know what he means, and I'm not insane. For the first time in my life, I know exactly what I want. I'm not afraid of putting a name to what Rose is to me. I realize that whether I said it or not, I always knew. I've always known what I wanted us to be.

"Wait," Owen says, pushing off the wall and crossing his arms over his chest. "I'm not judging, but how do you go from crashing at my place to marriage? Does she even know what happened?"

"She knows, and she wanted to help, but I sent her away. She went to visit her parents and said she'd be back last night. I wanted to give her time to process everything on her own so that I could do the same," I explain.

Dalton sneers disapprovingly. "You do realize that's not how a marriage works, right?"

"I know, but we're not married yet. I wanted Rose to be sure she knew what she was signing up for."

"And how do you know she's sure?" Owen asks. "You haven't spoken to her since she came home."

"I don't," I say simply. "But I do know that we have something worth fighting for. I've made up my mind. I want her with me. I could use some support picking out a ring, though."

Owen looks at Dalton, then back at me. "How much time do we have?"

"Today," I responded.

"Well, since there seems to be no talking you out of it, let's go pick out a ring," Dalton says.

I didn't realize ring shopping would be so complicated. I thought I'd go in, find a ring, and that would be the end of it, but it took nearly an hour to find one that spoke to me.

Once we're back at Dalton's, Owen and I leave, and I drop him off at his house on the way home. I pull up in the driveway with a massive smile on my face. I feel lighter, happier now that I can see a future.

I stare at the three-carat diamond encased in a platinum band one last time before tucking it back inside the box, stuffing it into my pocket, and getting out of my truck. I'm not nervous as I thought I'd be. I do pause at the door to compose myself and try to wipe the silly grin off of my face so that I don't ruin the surprise.

I had planned on proposing tonight, but the guys talked me into waiting a few days. They had this whole idea about making a grand gesture somewhere where her friends could be a part of it. I liked the idea of everyone bearing witness to something that will only happen once for us, so I agreed.

I open the door and step inside. The last conversation Rose and I had still lingered in the air, cold and raw, wiping the smile off of my face. A stark reminder that I pushed her away, and just because she's back, it doesn't mean she came back to me.

I step further inside, peering down the hall. Her door that used to be open and welcoming is closed, just as it was before she left.

Maybe she needs more time, I think. Or perhaps she's decided that we were a big mistake.

I can't expect her to bounce back so quickly. Can I?

I walk up to the door and stop, attempting a knock but stopping just before my knuckle touched it. Instead, my hand opens as I lay my palm flat against it. I rest my forehead on the door and close my eyes for a moment. I know she's there. I can feel her presence. I can always feel when she's near.

I remove my head and hand from the door, stepping away, and into the guest bedroom, closing the door softly behind me. I pull the small box from my pocket and tuck it safely inside my duffle bag, where I know she won't find it. Then, I sit on the bed with my back against the headboard and pull out my phone.

Finding Rose's name, I open up the text and type out a message.

Me: Petals, are you there?

I wait several seconds with the dots appearing and disappearing and reappearing again. It seems silly because Rose is in the next room, and I could just go to her, but this seems safer. This way, we can communicate without temptation staring us in the face.

I smile when her message finally comes through.

Petals: I'm here.

Me: Are you still with me?

Petals: I want to be.

I stare at her response that seems to have an invisible *but* attached at the end. I'm afraid to ask—afraid to bear off-topic. I don't want to know what that empty space holds, so I ignore it for now.

Me: Truth for a truth?

Petals: Always.

Me: I'm still falling, Petals, and I never want to stop.

The dots on my screen go through another cycle of uncertainty, my heart starting and stopping with each wave before she responds.

Petals: I think we should take a step back. I think we need to talk.

I blink at her response, unsure if I'm reading it right—not entirely sure of what it means. I certainly didn't expect it. Here I am ready to move forward, and she wants to take a step back. This wasn't in the plans. Not in my plans.

How do I even respond to that? Part of me wants to be mad at her for springing this on me now. But the other part—the part that sent her away—understands her reluctance. I go with the latter, deciding that's the only side with a shot at reasoning with her.

Me: Okay.

Petals: Tomorrow.

I throw the phone on the bed beside me, frustrated with myself. This is all my fault. I think as I press my palms together in front of my face, my pointers sliding up and down the side of my nose. I can't lose Rose too. I'll give her tonight, but I refuse to let her pull away from me. I couldn't fight for Jasper because he was never mine to begin with, but this situation with Rose is different. She has always been a part of me, even when all I knew was her name.

I stare at the ceiling for a few minutes, then pick my phone up and send our manager, Justin, a message. If anyone can pull off what I want with such short notice, it's him.

-

Chapter Twenty-Five

Rose

My cowardice kicked in, and I left home earlier than usual this morning. I couldn't face Luke, knowing what I have to do. It would've been all I could think of for the entire day at work.

I finally got the guy, but I'm not entirely sure if he's with me. Luke shutting me out made me think, and it brought up old memories from my past relationship. We ended so suddenly that I felt my life was ripped away from me. I've moved on since, and piecing my life back together wasn't all that hard, but a loss is a loss. It still hurt. That's why I'm procrastinating with Luke because I know it won't be as easy this time. What I feel for him runs miles deeper.

I sigh, leaning back in my new chair in my new office. It's only been a few days that I've been here. With everything going on, it hasn't sunk in yet. I'm enjoying it, but it feels like I'm living someone else's life. My whole life feels like a warped dream right now—one that I never thought possible. I just wish that it would level out so that I can see my way through it. It would be nice to catch a glimpse of the type of dream it would become. Whether it turns into a nightmare or a fairytale. Whether I'll want to wake up or drown in it.

I look across the hall through the glass door to Joselyn's office and outside her window overlooking the city. I can't see what's below, but even the sky's view from here is spectacular compared to what I was used to before. Her office is vacant at the moment due to my eagerness to escape this morning. It's nice having her this close again. It's like old times but on a different floor. She was right about one thing. The view outside my window is not all that great, but on the plus side, my job is better, and my office is bigger—more space and furniture than I know what to do with.

I glance at the comfy sofa and coffee table to my left— a good and bad idea I've decided. It's supposed to make guests feel more comfortable, more willing to spill the beans, but every time I look at it, I want to lie down and take a nap, which is why I've only sat on the thing once.

"Someone's here early this morning." Joselyn walks into my office, belly first with a smile too bright for this time of the morning.

My lips curve into a smile. "Hey. I see you and baby star finally decided to show up," I joke.

Her hands instinctively move to her belly as she comes closer, stopping in front of my desk.

"What are you doing later?" She asks, and her eyes seem to twinkle as she speaks.

I shrug. Aside from going home and possibly breaking up with Luke. "Nothing. Why?" I ask, squinting my eyes at her. "What do you have in mind?"

Joselyn's behavior is oddly suspicious. Usually, I'm the one asking her to go places. She's definitely up to something, but I don't question it.

"Well, since you asked nicely," she says, sitting on the corner of my desk. "I want to surprise a certain someone with something," she says, wiggling her brows.

I let out a small chuckle. "A certain someone, huh?" I ask. She and Dalton are ridiculously cute in the way they behave.

She snickers. "Yeah, but I have to go somewhere first. I figured since Dalton's busy later, and if you were free, today would be perfect. So…" she drags out. "Will you come?"

It takes me all of five seconds to decide. I don't care where we're going as long as it gives me an excuse to avoid Luke for a little while longer.

"Sure. Count me in," I answer.

"Great," she responds, giddily clapping her hands and standing. "It'll be just like old times. Except," she pauses, pointing her fingers at her belly.

I laugh at that. Joselyn refuses to say anything that may be considered negative directed at the baby. It's sweet but still funny.

"Can't wait," I say honestly. I want to know what all of the fuss is about.

After work, Joselyn insists that I ride with her and Dean to wherever it is we're going. So, I leave my car in the parking garage until we're done.

Joselyn and I get in the back seat of the truck as if it's not a strange thing to do. I've been escorted by Luke's bodyguard before, so it's not foreign to me, but this feels different because none of the guys are here. I don't know if I could get used to someone carrying me around everywhere I go all the time.

I glance at Joselyn, who seems to have fallen into the life with little effort. I wonder if Dalton is overreacting because of the baby or if he's just overreacting in general. I mean, is this really necessary? Then I glance at Dean, who's sworn to protect the guys with his own life. I suppose the baby is Dalton's life now, and also Joselyn. She's probably grateful for the added protection. But… My thoughts trail off as I lean closer to Joselyn, whispering in her ear.

"Does he know how to keep a secret?" I ask, nodding toward Dean in the driver's seat.

A glance at the rearview mirror lets me know that my whisper wasn't so quiet. Dean is watching me, his lips curved into his cheeks. I straighten, clearing my throat and smiling back at him, slightly embarrassed.

Joselyn giggles. "This isn't our first rodeo. Right, Dean?" The two of them share a knowing glance as he answers, "Nope," and I wonder what other mischiefs she's had him involved in. "He can keep a secret. They all can," she assures me with a wink. "As long as it doesn't endanger our lives," she adds.

Silence fills the truck as Dean pulls away. I try to direct my thoughts to something, anything but Luke, but it's no use. My mind automatically drifts to him, and I wonder if I'll ever be able to think of anything ever again without thinking of him first.

I seem to be the only one in the truck who thinks the ride is long. Each time I glance at Joselyn, that silly smile is still plastered on her face. When I think of a security guard, I think serious, but Dean seems to have jumped on the wagon, too, with the fixed smirk he's wearing.

When we finally reach our destination, all I can do is stare. My forehead wrinkled in confusion, and only one question comes to mind. I stare at the building in front of us, then turn my attention to Joselyn.

"What on earth could you possibly need from here?" I ask her.

Her response is immediate. "If I tell you, it will ruin the surprise." She stares at me for a moment, then adds, "Come on. We don't have long," as if it's the most normal thing in the world.

Chapter Twenty-Six

Luke

Justin is a miracle worker. He came through for me. He spent the morning calling in favors and making promises that the guys and I agreed to, of course. I only hope that our efforts are not in vain. I hope that I haven't blown it with Rose.

I ditched the notion of something elaborate and went with simple. When the idea occurred to me last night, I didn't give it a second thought. Rose and I could use a fresh start. We deserve a do-over—to go back to the place where it all started.

Highschool.

The evening air is calming, the sun just starting to lower from the sky.

It's perfect.

Justin talked the principal into letting us visit the school grounds once school let out and all of the kids were gone. We're not allowed inside, but that's fine because that's not where Rose and I began.

As soon as my foot touches the perfectly manicured grass, it all comes rushing back to me, and I smile, remembering the day so clearly.

Luke - Six Years Ago
I stepped outside the school, my eyes immediately roaming the grounds for her, just as I'd done every day since the first time I ever saw her. When I found her, I smiled and looked away, pretending that my day hadn't just been made.

There was something about her that was different from all the other girls, or maybe it was just me. Whatever the reason, I was drawn to her. She was younger, a freshman, I think, and I knew I'd catch hell if the guys or anyone found out how I felt about her. Seniors didn't fall for the underclassmen. Though, some pretended to for obvious reasons. I didn't know what I wanted from that girl, but a roll in the sack wasn't it. Well, that wasn't all I wanted.

I knew that her name was Rose. That she was not dating anyone. I knew that her hair was dark and her skin was perfect, and she had the most beautiful smile I'd ever seen. She had a personality that would make any guy think twice, but I think that's the thing that drew me to her the most.

I walked to our usual spot outside the school with Dalton and Owen, posting up against the building. They'd been going on about something since we stepped outside, but I can't exactly say what as my attention was elsewhere.

"Luke," I heard Dalton say.

"Huh?" I asked, completely clueless.

"Did you hear what I said?" He asked, then repeated himself. "You're always daring us to do crazy shit. I think it's time for you to pay up."

I looked at him and smirked, ready for whatever they had in mind. I wasn't afraid of a challenge.

"Okay," I shrugged. "Bring it on," I said smugly.

His smile turned devious, but it still didn't frighten me.

I cocked a brow, waiting. Then finally, Dalton said, "That girl over there, the one with the red shirt on. I dare you to ask her out."

I followed his eyes to the same girl I had been trying to avoid. The same girl who made my stomach feel funny when I gazed at her. I wasn't afraid of any challenge they could've thrown at me, except for that one. Walking up to her wouldn't have been like approaching just any girl. Rose was different, but I had to keep my feelings in check. I couldn't let anyone know—not even my friends.

I swallowed down the lump in my throat, keeping my smile and cool demeanor intact, and said, "Okay."

Rose glanced in my direction as I approached, and I couldn't tell if she was nervous or annoyed. I, for one, was nervous, but I didn't dare let it show. I walked right up to her, unsure if I was interrupting anything, and at the same time, not caring. Being that close to her and seeing the warm caramel of her eyes, I knew that I wanted her. I knew *that if she said yes, I wouldn't care how anyone else would feel. Something about how she returned my stare gave me the strength to blurt out the question that I was afraid to ask.*

"Can I take you out sometime? On a date?" I asked.

Rose's eyes widened, then her mouth opened. What I thought was going to be a yes, turned into a laugh—a seemingly uncontrollable laugh.

I showed no emotion when I nodded and backed away, except for the smile I kept fixed on my face. I turned back toward my friends, still carrying that fake smile. I had done what I was dared to do. I had won, but in the pit of my stomach, I felt as if I'd just lost everything. I couldn't believe she'd turned me down. I was heartbroken.

The guys laughed like it was the funniest thing, and I guess it was. I guess payback was a bitch.

Present Time

"Daydreaming again?" Owen asks, his palm landing on my shoulder.

I grunt out a laugh.

"They should be here any minute," Dalton says, walking up beside us. "Josie's message said Rose has no clue," he says of his wife.

We're standing in the same area we always stood in high school, and there's a plush grey carpet in the spot where Rose stood that day. I didn't bring flowers or candy, and I didn't get all dressed up because I wanted it to be as close to authentic as possible.

My heart stops when Rose rounds the corner. She's even more beautiful than the last time that I saw her. Still in her work attire—black pants and beige top. Hair a little frizzed but beautiful.

She looks around confused, then her eyes land on me, and she stops. Joselyn guides her over to the carpet square and whispers something into her ear. I don't know what she said to get Rose here, but I'm grateful. Joselyn motions for Dalton and Owen to follow her so that Rose and I are left alone.

Once they're out of sight, I square my shoulders and walk toward Rose. She has that same look on her face—the one where I can't decipher what she's thinking. Her eyes hold mine until the point when I reach her.

"Rose," I say her name.

She looks away from me, and the loss of contact steals my breath. I recite in my head over and over again. *This is not the end. It's just the beginning.*

I open my mouth to say more when her eyes return to mine, but she cuts me off before I can speak.

"I have to say something," she starts. "I know what I said, Luke, but I can't do this anymore."

My heart drops into the pit of my stomach. I shake my head no, but she acts as if I'm not and continues.

"I need to say this before I lose my nerve," she says, swallowing deeply. "If having your son with you is what you want, I could have dealt with that. I would've helped you through it."

I can do nothing but stare as she speaks of us in the past tense.

"I could even deal with you being gone for weeks at a time because it's your job. What I can't deal with is not knowing what we are—being afraid to let a title slip for fear of losing you. I can't be a blank line on your roster forever. I want more, Luke. And I know that's not what you signed up for, so I'm giving you an out."

Rose turns away from me, her sniffles piercing my heart. Her words throw me, and I forget everything that I had planned to say.

"Hey," I step closer, pulling her back against my chest. "You were always more to me than a blank line, Rose. Don't you know that? Can't you feel it?" I pause and press a kiss to the back of her head, tightening my arms around her. "I never wanted you to be just my Rose, or my baby, or my girlfriend." I turn her to face me, cupping her face in my palms. "You," I say, my gaze determined to convince her. "You are the most important person in my life. Have been since the day we met. And I hope that you always will be."

Tears begin to fall from her eyes, and I wipe them away. I kiss her salt-stained lips, needing her to feel what I feel. This is not how I'd imagined this would play out. Rose was willing to let me go, and for what? A title? A stupid stipulation that I'd set before I knew what we'd become.

She covers her face with her hands, blocking me. I fall to one knee and take her hand in mine, but she squeezes her eyes shut.

"Rose, look at me, please, Petals." I hadn't realized how much she'd been hurting.

She opens her eyes, tears still threatening to fall, and her gaze locks with mine. I pull the ring from my pocket that I'd planned on giving her.

"Since I met you, I have done everything that I said I wouldn't do, and I don't see the point in stopping now. I saved the best title for you if you'll have it. The only one that matters."

"What?" Her free hand flies to her chest, her breathing rapid, eyes wide open, and clouded.

"Will you marry me, Rose?" My fingers pause with the ring poised at her ring finger, waiting for her answer. "Will you be my wife?"

Rose stills, her eyes moving from me to the ring and back. Then I see it, that other expression taking over—the one where she looks like she wants to laugh, and I realize she was telling the truth. She didn't laugh in my face to be cruel all those years ago. She did it because she was nervous. So, I ask again, making sure she knows this is not a joke or some stupid dare.

"Marry me, Petals? And I promise you'll never have to wonder again. You'll always know who you are and how much you mean to me."

Her head begins to nod. Then she says, "Yes." I slip the ring onto her finger, then stand and lift her into my arms.

With her legs wrapped around my back and arms around my neck, I press my lips to hers, kissing her feverishly, like I'd been starved for weeks instead of days. I touch my forehead to hers when we pull apart, letting it sink in.

Rose agreed to be my wife, and though the proposal didn't go as planned, it was perfect—better than I could've imagined.

Rose lowers her feet to the ground, dragging her hand down my chest. Her eyes bore into mine as if they're asking if I'm sure.

I place a tender kiss on her lips, answering, "I've never been more sure about anything."

A rough hand claps my shoulder at the same time Rose is ripped away from me.

I hear Joselyn say to Rose, "What is it you always used to say to me? That was so hot." Then they laugh.

"That was kind of hot," Owen responds. "But you had us scared for a minute there."

A few minutes later, I see the principal waiting by the gate, and I take that as a cue that it's time to leave. His back is facing us as we approach the gate and exit, but we don't get far before he says her name.

Rose.

Everyone stops and turns to face him like he'd said all of our names at once. Rose's eyes widen in shock, her grip on my hand loosening, and all I can think is, *not again. Can't I have just one thing for myself?* Then the second thought leaps forward. *How the hell does he know her name?*

"Todd?" Rose eyes the principal curiously. "What are you doing here?" She asks.

His smile is bittersweet when he responds, "I work here. I'm the principal."

"You two know each other?" I ask them, and Rose looks at me.

"This is Todd," she says as if the name means something to me. When she realizes her mistake, she adds, "My ex."

Oh, that guy. I think—the one who hurt her. I'm torn between pummeling him and thanking him again for making this possible. I wonder if he knew it was her when he agreed.

"You agreed to this? Did you know?" Rose asks, and Todd nods.

"I felt... I wanted you to know how sorry I am." His arm rises toward her, then stops and drops back to his side. He glances at me nervously and back to Rose. "I'm glad you found happiness."

I can't read Rose's expression, so it's hard to know what she feels at the moment.

She stares for a few seconds, then says, "Thanks, I guess."

An awkward silence falls over us. Then Rose looks at me. "Do you mind if we have a moment?" She asks.

It's not that I don't trust her. I'm worried about this guy hurting her again. I want to say no, but something in her eyes tells me she wants this, needs this.

I kiss her temple, wanting nothing more than to stay. "I'll wait by the car."

We move away from Rose and Todd, leaving them to catch up. Our friends get into the truck with Dean and leave shortly after. Russell waits patiently inside the third vehicle while I lean against my truck, waiting for Rose.

I can't hear what she and Todd are saying, but I watch their actions closely. I notice that Rose doesn't smile once. Her expression remains neutral the entire time. Todd seems to be doing most of the talking, and I wonder if that's what their relationship was like. Was he controlling? Was everything about him all the time? Did he ever ask Rose what she wanted?

I imagine he didn't because if he had, none of this would be happening. He would've been where I am—happy with Rose. He wouldn't have let her go. He was a fool for that, and I'm the lucky man that gets to reap the benefits of his mistake.

Ten minutes pass before Rose glances at me, and I finally hear a clear sentence.

"We really should be going, Todd. Guess I'll be seeing you around. Thanks again for this," Rose says as she backs toward me then turn around.

Todd nods, watching Rose as she walks away. It's not a creepy gaze. It's more like regret, and for some reason, that makes me smile on the inside. Then he looks at me, giving me a curt nod.

I nod back just as Rose reaches me.

Rose gets into my truck's passenger seat, and I climb in on the driver's side. We pull away, leaving Todd to lock up, with Russell following behind us.

The ride home is quiet, but Rose smiles the entire time. I don't bother asking what she and Todd spoke about. I'm just glad she got what she needed. When I park the truck, I turn, watching the glow bouncing off of her.

"Do you know how happy I am?" She asks me, keeping her eyes straight.

"How happy are you?" I ask.

She finally looks at me, the smile still on her face.

"Nothing could make this night more perfect," she says. "I thought I needed closure, but I didn't. I thought that if I ever saw him again, it would be different—that I would feel something, but I felt nothing. All thanks to you," she says. "You have made me the happiest woman in the world tonight," she says, sliding across the seat toward me.

I cup the side of her face, accepting her answer but not satisfied.

"Not just tonight, Petals. Every night for the rest of our lives," I amend.

Chapter Twenty-Seven

Two Weeks Later

Luke

Nervous doesn't begin to describe what I'm feeling. I clearly hadn't thought everything through before I asked Rose to marry me. Don't get me wrong. It was one of the best decisions I've ever made, but now I have to meet her parents. The thought alone had me driving twice as slow as I usually do to get here.

I shouldn't be nervous. I'm used to meeting all kinds of people. I don't see why this would be different, except it is.

A not-so-crazy thought occurs that maybe I should've met Rose's parents before the proposal. What if they hate me for not including them?

The last time Rose saw her parents, I had sent her away.

"Luke," Rose's sweet voice breaks through my haze. She places her hand on my arm, and I turn my head in her direction. Rose holds back a laugh then says, "We talked about this. My parents are looking forward to meeting you. They're more nervous about this than you."

I glance in the rearview mirror, thinking maybe I should've brought Russell along with us.

Rose laughs. "You're ridiculous. You don't need protection from my parents," she says, reading my mind. "Let's go inside before you change your mind."

Before I can object, Rose opens her door and exits the truck. She walks toward the house, her hips moving from side to side. I watch her for a few seconds, all thoughts of meeting her parents temporarily suspended. She knows exactly what to do to get me to stop thinking so much. Then I get out of the truck and jog to catch up to her.

I give Rose a devilish look when we reach the front door letting her know she will have to pay for her actions now that she's sent my thoughts south.

"Don't give me that look," she says. "You couldn't decide, so I did it for you."

She rings the doorbell, then smirks while wiggling her brows. I open my mouth to respond but quickly shut it when the door swings open.

"Welcome," comes a cheery greeting.

I turn my head toward the voice and get a clear view of what my Rose will be like when she's older.

Rose clears her throat next to me. "Hey," she says, bumping against my side. "She's already spoken for."

"Sorry," I say to her mom after realizing I'd been staring. "I'm Luke," I add, holding my hand out to her.

Rose's mom steps forward, threading her arm through mine. "You can call me Lilly," she says, escorting me into the house ahead of Rose.

"Hey," I hear Rose exclaim behind us as the click of the door closing hits my ears.

"Don't worry about her," Lilly says. "I hear she has the rest of her life to spend with you," she says pointedly, then giggles.

Something about the way she says it calms me, and I laugh too. "Yes, ma'am. She does," I responded. I thought she'd be upset, but she seems fine with the idea of me marrying her daughter.

"Where's dad?" Rose asks.

Lilly glances over her shoulder, answering, "You know your father."

"Yardwork," comes Rose's response and a quiet chuckle.

"I'll let Rose give you the tour later," Lilly says as we continue to the back door. "Leo is anxious to meet you. Rose has never brought a guy home before."

"Mom," Rose whines.

"Well, it's true," Lilly says, waving Rose's comment away. "Anyway, Leo is excited about adding another male to the family," she adds, stopping when we reach the door. She lets go of my arm and looks at me. "If you have any reservations, speak now."

I almost ask her if she's serious because the last minute or so didn't seem real. It's not at all how I thought this meeting would play out.

"There's no way I'm ever backing out," I respond. "I promised Rose a lifetime," I say, taking Rose's hand in mine.

Lilly glances at our joined hands and smiles, accepting my answer. Then she opens the door, and we step outside.

"Rose, Luke, you're finally here," Rose's father says as we move toward him. He behaves as if he's known me for a long time. He holds out his dirt-coated hand, and I take it, not wanting to be rude. "Leo," he introduces, a chuckle following. He looks at Rose. "I wasn't sure he'd shake my filthy hand. I like him." Then he looks back at me.

Rose certainly didn't steal her mannerisms. Her parents are just as forward as she is and equally as polite.

"Luke, sir," I finally responded. "Good to meet you."

"Likewise, son."

Son.

It's weird hearing a man that's not my father call me that.

A tinge of sadness hits me for a moment, thinking of Jasper. If I had taken him away from the only father he's ever known and suddenly began calling him son, I imagine it would've felt even weirder for him.

"So, Luke, what are your intentions with my daughter?"

"Dad," Rose objects, and he glances her way without an ounce of apology.

"What? I wouldn't be a good father if I didn't ask. And Luke is well known for being a play..."

"Dad!" Rose objects again.

I chuckle, even though his unspoken words stung a bit. He's obviously been doing his research. I want to assure them that most of what they've read isn't true, but my words probably won't make much difference. Leo seems like a man who needs to see it to believe it.

"Don't believe the crap you read in the tabloids," Rose continues, cutting her eyes at me briefly, and I'm grateful for the suggestion. "Unless you confirm it with me first," she adds with a smirk.

"Alright, alright," Leo chuckles. "I won't grill you, son. My baby girl seems happy, and she brought you home to meet us, so that has to count for something. Just try not to break her heart," he says, staring straight into my eyes.

It's not an unusual request. I can't promise that I won't break her heart because I'm sure I will, unintentionally, at some point, but I *can* try. I can try not to hurt her, and if I do, I can promise to make it right.

"You have my word," I respond.

"Good," he says, gripping my shoulder between his dirty fingers. "I just have one more important question."

"Anything you want to know," I say, trying not to glance at his hand on my shoulder and thinking about the shower I'll need when this is over. Oddly, I'm not even irritated by his actions. I'm mostly confused about what's happening.

Leo's expression turns serious as he asks, "How do you feel about getting dirty?"

I stare for a moment, caught off guard by his question. Leo lifts his hands, wiggling his fingers in the air. When his question finally registers, I laugh, and they join in with me.

"I'm okay with that," I finally respond.

I decide, at that moment, that Rose's parents are cool. It's refreshing being in the presence of a normal family.

Rose squeezes my hand and smiles up at me. I smile back, tightening my hand around hers.

I can't believe how lucky I am to have her.

I can't believe I was willing to let her go.

Epilogue

1 Year Later

Luke

I gave Russell the night off, knowing Rose and I would be safe at the beach house. It's been a long three days without my wife—three days of fans and being on the road, and abstinence. Tonight, I want her all to myself. I admit I'm a little jealous of Cadence, which turns out is her vibrator, but as stand-ins go, I'd rather *it* fills in rather than some other guy.

Rose and I have been married for three months, and I have to say that I'm enjoying the honeymoon phase. I get what all the hype is about. I didn't have to give up anything to be with her. I gained a partner, lover, and friend.

We had a small wedding with only a few of our closest friends and family at the beach house I'd bought for us last year. I guess you could call it wishful thinking or presumptuous, but even then, deep down, I knew what I wanted. I never stood a chance with Rose.

Rose hasn't settled on a home for us yet. So, we're still staying at her rental home until she decides. I'm okay with whatever she chooses as long as we're together. For now, we use the beach house as our home away from home as the commute to work each day for Rose would be too taxing.

Tonight, we're alone, and I plan to take full advantage of the privacy this place provides. I had Russell help me set up a tent near the water for us before he left. A bottle of wine and a few other things await us inside. All I need now is Rose.

I enter the bedroom, and my eyes land on Rose. She's lying on the bed facing the headboard, flipping through a magazine. Her white sundress's tail is at the start of her thighs, giving me a full view of her legs. Her calves are raised in the air moving back and forth, toes adorning that dreadfully sexy red that I love to hate. I'm willing to bet that she chose that color to get a reaction out of me.

"Checking out the competition?" I ask, stopping next to the bed.

Her gaze flits from the magazine to me. "Yep," she answers, a smile creeping onto her face.

"Anything interesting?" I ask, crossing my arms over my chest.

"Oh, you know, the usual," she says, tossing the magazine aside and standing. "Musician meets journalist. Musician falls in love and gets married." She unwraps my arms and steps into them, placing her palms on my chest.

"Hmm," I sigh, tightening my arms around her. "Is that all?"

Her mouth twists as her eyes rise in thought. She tweaks her brow. Then her gaze returns to me.

"Almost forgot the baby. Can't forget the baby," she says, playfully.

I chuckle at that. "Is that so?"

Rose and I have discussed children and decided when it happens, it happens. It hasn't yet, but according to the tabloids, we have a bun in the oven already. All it took was a photo of Rose in a too-big shirt for speculation to circulate.

"Mmhm," she nods.

"Well," I say, squeezing her ass and jerking her against me. "Maybe we should put forth more effort, Petals." I graze her bottom lip with my teeth, then let go. "Wouldn't want them to say we didn't try hard enough once they find out it's not true."

"No. We wouldn't want that," she agrees with hooded eyes.

Rose tilts her chin up, practically begging me to kiss her, and I almost do. Our lips are a breath away. I lick my lips on the precipice of giving in. Then I remember the tent and pull away.

"Not yet," I say, brushing my thumb over her cheek. "Come on. I have a surprise for you."

Rose pouts her disappointment, adding, "Should I bring Cadence?"

I lean close to her ear at the mention of that *thing*. I know she only said it to get a reaction out of me, and she succeeded. The thought of her thirst being quenched by anyone or anything other than me is one I don't particularly enjoy.

"Trust me. You won't need it for a while. As long as I'm here, every need and every desire you have will be fulfilled."

She sucks in a breath. Then she lets me guide her outside to the beach.

The tent is huge—one fit for a camp with just enough height to stand.

Rose looks inside, her eyes widening. "When did you? How did you?" She asks.

"Russell helped me out before he left," I answered.

"Protective and handy," Rose says, impressed.

The carpet square that I'd used to propose to her last year lay at the entrance to the tent. Rose and I sat there while watching the sunset.

"Still as beautiful as the first time I saw it," Rose says next to me while looking toward the now invisible horizon. Then her head turns, and her eyes find mine. "Do you remember what you said to me that night?" She asks.

I remember that night and every night that we've spent together since. Even now, my words remain true. I rub my thumb across the back of her hand that I'm holding.

"You're still my wonder, Petals."

Rose smiles, sending a jolt straight to my heart. She lets go of my hand and begins backing into the tent.

"Well, in case you're wondering what I'm thinking now," she says. "I've missed my husband."

She disappears inside, and I follow her like a beast on the prowl. She opens her legs wide, and I pause, momentarily stunned by the view. She lay bare, wet, and ready for me. My dick twitches in my shorts, begging to be released.

"You're a naughty girl, Petals," I smirk, regaining my control. I lift her leg and place a kiss on her ankle. Then put it over my shoulder. "But I didn't wait three days just to rush into this. I need to kiss you." I run my hand the length of her leg, and her body shivers beneath my touch. "And touch you." I dip my head down and run my tongue over her clit. "And taste you." I flick my tongue over her again, then lap at her entire center. "In case you're wondering what I'm thinking."

"Luke," she pleads.

"I missed making love to my wife, but I also miss the details that come before it." I push her dress up over her breasts, reaching up and pinching her nipple between my fingers. "The way your breath hitches." I crane my neck to kiss the spot right below her belly button. "And your skin heats."

I kiss my way down until I'm at her center. My tongue trails over her again, this time pulling her clit into my mouth and sucking. She moans, and my tongue dips inside of her. I grip her thigh, my nose teasing and my tongue devouring her warm offering.

"Lucas," she breathes out, calling me by my given name. The urgency in her voice tells me she's more than ready.

I stop my actions and take off my shorts. My eyes trail over Rose's entire body, perfect and all mine. Then I lower myself on top of her and ease inside. The first hit of her is always the most sensitive, forcing me to pause and catch my breath.

Fuck. I think, closing my eyes for a moment.

Her body molds to mine, pulsating around me as I begin to move. Her hips rise each time I drive into her, urging me to go deeper. It's hard not to let go when I'm deep inside of her, but I don't. I hold on between untamed kisses and throaty moans until Rose's body quivers and tightens around me—until her eyes roll and her grip on my shoulder becomes taut. Then I bury myself to the hilt and let go.

A few seconds pass before I roll over beside Rose. She's staring up at the top of the tent, and I'm staring at her and the rapid movement of her chest. She turns onto her side facing me, and I reach over to brush her hair over her shoulder.

"Sex on the beach," she says, and I chuckle. "I love it," she adds.

"Good thing we own the place," I respond, leaning over to kiss her.

Things with Jeremy and Marcia are still tense after a year, but at least we can be in the same space now for the sake of Jasper.

I kept my word and didn't fight them, but made it clear that I wanted to be a part of his life. So, I've been spending time with him on occasion, as his uncle Luke of course. Looking into his face that's a clear image of mine is still hard. I suppose that's a wound that will never heal.

Rose is even warming up to him. I sometimes wonder what our life would've been like had I fought for Jasper. Would we even have a life together? Then I push the thoughts away, remembering nothing good could come of it.

Jeremy sent a text as Rose and I were leaving the beach house this morning. He wanted me to know that they were having lunch at mom and dad's today if we wanted to come. He started sending messages a few months back, and at first, I ignored them. Everything was still so fresh and hard to swallow, but Rose helped me through it. She didn't try to push me. She was just there, and one day she told me something that finally clicked—something that I'd already known but needed to hear again. She said, *"We'll never be complete until you deal with it. I know it's hard, but it's not about you. It's about Jasper, and that little boy needs you in his life, whether he knows it or not."* She said we couldn't get married until I made an effort. I love Rose, but that—her words—giving up someone she loves for someone she doesn't know. I loved her even more at that moment.

Rose joins our hands together as we walk into my parent's home. She gives me a reassuring smile like she always does when we visit. My mom greets us at the door, and we walk into the kitchen. As soon as I round the corner, Jasper's face lights up, and he runs over to me.

"Uncle Luke!" he shouts, and regardless of the title, my heart swells.

"Hey, sport," I respond, ruffling his hair. Jasper hates it when I do that, but I do it anyway because that's what uncles are for.

"I got a new car. Wanna see?" He asks, excitement filling his voice.

I chuckle, glancing over at Jeremy, who shakes his head. It's because of me that Jasper is ecstatic about toy car collecting. Jeremy was annoyed with the idea until I convinced him it would be good for Jasper to focus some of his energy on something other than video games. We always enjoyed playing with cars growing up.

"Sure. Lead the way," I tell Jasper.

Jasper shows me his newest car, and I watch in wonder as he tells me about its features. He's a smart kid and so full of life. I kind of wish the day never comes when he learns the truth.

After we eat lunch, we go outside into the back yard. Mom, dad, and Marcia sit on the patio while Jeremy and Jasper play catch with a football.

I pull Rose aside, taking her to our new favorite spot—away from everyone else. We sit in the grass as we'd done the first time I brought her here, but this time is different. This time, I know I'll be okay because there's no threat of bad news popping up, and I still have her.

She looks over her shoulder at me from where she sits between my legs and smiles.

"Truth for a truth," she asks.

I smile back at her. "Always."

"I love you, Lucas Anders, and I'm so proud of the man that you are," she says.

"I love you too, Petals, and you'll always be my wonder," I respond, placing a simple kiss on her lips but wanting so much more.

Life, I've decided, is a series of beginnings and endings. We can make choices, but ultimately, we have no control over the outcome. I don't know what the future holds for Jasper, but I believe I chose right for him. I chose Rose for me, and she chose me for herself.

I'm content with my choices and refuse to think about what the outcome might be because it's out of my control. For now, I'm going to enjoy every breath and every moment because that's what living life is—being in the now.

I didn't count on any of this, but I'm grateful for it all. I believe Rose came into my life at the perfect time. She accepted my mess of a life and helped to refine it into something better than I ever could on my own.

    Because of Rose, I overcame my ridiculous avoidance of titles. I have a better understanding of what love truly is. It's about knowing when to take and when to give—accepting that's it's okay to do both with the right person. Because of her, I found Lucas, the man behind the music—son, brother, uncle, friend, and husband.

    So, if you asked me if I had any intentions of giving any of that up, I'd say no.

    And if you asked me, what's in a rose? I'd answer, my everything.

The End.

REFINED CADENCE

Acknowledgments

To my family,
Thank you for your patience and your ears and sound advice. I couldn't do this without you.

To my beta readers, Mary & Missy,
Thank you for your insight. You helped to make the finish product what it is. Your time is much appreciated, and I'm so blessed to have both of you on my team.

To my group, Parker's Angels
Thank you for being a part of my circle, for every comment, every like, every follow, and every share. It's nice to have a place to escape, and I have that with you.

As always, thank you from the bottom of my heart to the bloggers, authors, and everyone who had anything to do with this book's release. My words exist in the hands and hearts of many because of you.

Author's Note

Everything that anyone does, big or small, plays a huge part in an author's success. I appreciate you all so very much. Thanks for coming along with me on my journey. If you enjoyed reading my book, please consider posting a review on your preferred site; and don't forget to tell your friends about me.

Until Next Time

About The Author

Angela K. Parker is a country girl with a big heart. She's a South Carolina native with a passion for writing, reading, music, & math. When she's not engaged in any of the above, she's spending time with her family or catching up on the latest movies. She's always had a very active imagination. Now she's putting it to good use.

Other Works by The Author

Life & Love Series Duet
B1: A Life No Less Than Perfect
B2: A Love Fulfilled

Kind Series
B1: An Unexpected Kind
B2: A Callous Kind
B3: A Forgiving Kind

Motion Series
B1: Love In Motion
B2: Refined Cadence

Novellas
Emerald Runs Deep
The Miracle Within Me
Butter Pecan Dream
Beyond The Blueprint

Connect With The Author

Website: www.angelakparker.com
Facebook: www.facebook.com/angelaparkerauthor
Facebook Group: www.facebook.com/groups/parkersangels
Goodreads: www.goodreads.com/author/show/16881406.Angela_K_Parker
Newsletter Signup: http://eepurl.com/cI3h6H
Twitter: http://twitter.com/akpauthor
Instagram: http://www.instagram.com/angelaparkerauthor/
BookBub: https://www.bookbub.com/authors/angela-k-parker
Pinterest: http://www.pinterest.com/angelaparkerauthor/
Email: angelaparkerauthor@gmail.com

Printed in Great Britain
by Amazon